A galaxy OF Sea Stars

A galaxy OF Sea Stars

Jeanne Zulick Ferruolo

SQUARE
FISH

FARRAR STRAUS GIROUX · NEW YORK

SQUARE
FISH

An imprint of Macmillan Publishing Group, LLC
120 Broadway, New York, NY 10271
mackids.com

A GALAXY OF SEA STARS. Copyright © 2020 by Jeanne Zulick Ferruolo.
All rights reserved. Printed in the United States of America by
LSC Communications, Harrisonburg, Virginia.

Square Fish and the Square Fish logo are trademarks of Macmillan and
are used by Farrar Straus Giroux under license from Macmillan.

Our books may be purchased in bulk for promotional, educational, or business
use. Please contact your local bookseller or the Macmillan Corporate and
Premium Sales Department at (800) 221-7945 ext. 5442 or by email
at MacmillanSpecialMarkets@macmillan.com.

Library of Congress Cataloging-in-Publication Data

Names: Ferruolo, Jeanne Zulick, author.
Title: A galaxy of sea stars / Jeanne Zulick Ferruolo.
Description: | New York : Farrar Straus Giroux Books for Young
    Readers, 2020. | Summary: Izzy struggles with her parents'
    separation, starting middle school, and more, but especially the
    effect her friendship with her Muslim neighbor, Sitara, has on her
    best friends, Zelda and Piper.
Identifiers: LCCN 2019015954 | ISBN 978-1-250-76326-6 (paperback)
Subjects: | CYAC: Best friends—Fiction. | Friendship—Fiction. |
    Middle schools—Fiction. | Schools—Fiction. | Muslims—Fiction. |
    Afghans—United States—Fiction. | Immigrants—Fiction. |
    Family problems—Fiction.
Classification: LCC PZ7.1.F4697 Gal 2020 | DDC [Fic]—dc23
LC record available at https://lccn.loc.gov/2019015954

Originally published in the United States by Farrar Straus Giroux
First Square Fish edition, 2021
Book designed by Cassie Gonzales
Square Fish logo designed by Filomena Tuosto

3   5   7   9   10   8   6   4

LEXILE: 650L

With special thanks to
Hilla, Maria, Safia, Asma, Deyana & Nour,
whose courage, kindness, and brilliance
illuminate the universe

And for Paul, Andrew & Sophia,
who complete my galaxy

Chapter 1

On the day before Izzy Mancini started sixth grade, she waded through the shallow water of Oceanside Pond carrying a clipboard, a weighted string, and a summer full of worry.

From the bow of her anchored skiff, Flotsam watched patiently. His salty wet fur sparkled in the afternoon sun.

"One more measurement," she told him as she lowered the weight, attached to its long knotted string, into the salt pond. It settled to the silty floor with a soft *poof*, causing a hermit crab to scurry away. Izzy pinched the string where it met the water's surface, then pulled it out, counting the knots.

"Almost three feet deep," she told Flotsam as she recorded the number next to its GPS coordinate on her map. When she finished, she waded back to the skiff, holding the clipboard safely above her head. Water lapped at the frayed cuffs of her shorts.

At mean low tide, each day since she and her dad and Starenka had moved to the marina, Izzy measured a new section of Oceanside Pond. With everyone and everything in her world changing, mapping the pond had become a way for Izzy to make at least one thing stand still.

At the back of the skiff, she tucked her maps carefully into their patchwork bag, then checked her phone for the millionth time, hoping to discover a new clue inside Zelda's text. But no matter how many times she swiped open the screen, the message stayed the same:

meet at sea star HQ @3:00 i know what to do

She tossed the phone inside her patchwork bag, which she slung over her shoulder.

"It's time, Flotsam," she said. "Let's go."

On the word *go*, he leapt from the boat in a black-and-white streak, splashing Izzy before scampering onto the pond's rocky shore. She shook her head as he disappeared inside thick green sea-rose bushes.

Oceanside Pond was a coastal lagoon. Three miles long, it was created by a barrier beach that protected it from the Atlantic Ocean. Izzy made her way onto the sandy path that led to the ocean side of that barrier, careful to avoid the rocks and shells hidden there by angry waves on stormier days.

She squinted at the hazy sun, shining in its new end-of-summer slant. She scowled. Izzy didn't like any ending, but the last day of summer was the worst ending of all.

It's Labor Day, she reminded herself. *Technically not the last day of summer, but an ending just the same.*

The bushes rustled and Flotsam popped out, grinning a goofy dog smile as if to say, *Surprise, I was here all along.* Izzy couldn't help but grin back.

As they emerged onto Brogee's Beach, the Atlantic roared its welcome. Its giant gray waves slapped the beach before sucking back sand and stone with a gravelly growl. Izzy wanted to cover her ears. Instead, she felt for the key tucked deep inside her pocket and held it tight in her fist. Somehow this small act comforted her. She took a deep breath, then continued down the beach, wishing she could have met her friends on the pond side instead.

Her bare feet sank into the hot sand as Flotsam trotted about—one moment falling behind to nose a clump of seaweed, the next racing ahead to chase a gull. Wagons, piled high with toys and chairs and kids, tipped from side to side as parents dragged them from the beach.

"Always first," she said to Flotsam as they reached their destination—a short, hollow concrete box that she and her best friends, Zelda and Piper, had dubbed the Sea Star Headquarters in a sacred ceremony when they were six.

According to her dad, the box was a relic from World War II. It had a square window that the girls used to decorate with seaweed curtains, and a circular opening on top that they could shimmy into. Back then, it was the perfect size for three best friends.

She adjusted her patchwork bag, then climbed onto

its "roof." The sun-warmed concrete felt rough and solid beneath her feet. Even though the girls couldn't fit inside anymore, it was still where they met to discuss important business. Right then, nothing was more important than their move to Shoreline Regional Middle School.

The new school brought in kids from four towns. Izzy's town, Seabury, was the smallest. Although she wouldn't see her schedule until the first day of school, it didn't stop her from imagining the worst. She worried that Zelda and Piper would be in the same classes while she was stuck with kids she didn't know. She agonized over being lost in long hallways, late to class, and surrounded by strangers. She envisioned herself scanning the cafeteria for a familiar face—only to eat alone. She had nightmares about missed homework, missed buses, and missed friends.

A loud whoop from a cluster of surfers brought her thoughts back to the beach. They looked like busy seals in their black wet suits as they took turns paddling and catching waves. She shuddered, remembering her own one-time attempt at surfing when she almost drowned. The roar of the ocean had filled her head then too. This memory was enough to make her want to cover her ears all over again.

"Hey!" Piper interrupted her thoughts. She walked toward Izzy, still wearing her soccer socks and carrying cleats.

"Hey." Izzy crossed her arms. "The ocean seems extra angry today, doesn't it?"

Piper shrugged. "I don't know. Offshore storm maybe?"

Izzy suddenly felt exposed. She jumped down into the hot sand, her patchwork bag slapping her leg.

"I can't believe summer's over and we barely got to hang out," Piper said.

"The move . . . you know . . . ," Izzy said. "Everyone's been real busy working at the marina and I had to help and—"

"Sure." Piper half smiled. "Well, we'll see each other every day now."

Izzy couldn't make herself smile back.

Piper stared into the ocean's gray waves. "We're still doing our annual back-to-school sleepover Saturday night at your house, right?"

"Oh . . . yeah. I forgot about that." Izzy swallowed hard. "Or we could do your house."

"How could you forget?" Piper fell back against the headquarters. "You were the one who made it a Sea Star annual tradition. We have to do your house— we've barely gotten to spend time at the marina. It will be so cool. Is your mom back yet?"

"We're picking her up from the eight o'clock ferry tonight." Izzy squinted across the sound to Block Island, where her mother had spent the summer working at her family's restaurant, Loretta's Kitchen. She could barely make out the North Lighthouse at the tip of Sandy Point.

Flotsam galloped toward them, crashing into Piper. She knelt down to pet him. "Hey, puppy, I've missed you!"

He reciprocated by shaking what seemed like a gallon of ocean from his shaggy black-and-white fur.

"I don't know why he has to wait until he's right next to people to do that."

Piper wiped her face with her sleeve. "I needed a shower anyway," she said, laughing.

Flotsam grinned his silly dog grin.

"I almost forgot," Piper said. "My mother told me to ask you when is a good time to give your mom all the PTO stuff."

"I'll ask her tonight."

"Text me what she says," Piper said as she picked seaweed from Flotsam's fur.

"So what do you think Zelda's message means? Do you think she figured out how we can stay together in middle school?" Izzy asked.

"I hope so." Piper looked at her watch. "She better get here soon. I have to be home by four to meet my new tutor."

"Already? School hasn't even started."

"You know my mom." Piper tucked her black curls behind her ears.

Another loud *whoop!* came from the direction of the ocean. The girls turned to watch Zelda riding a wave while sending air high fives to them. She'd been surfing all along.

Zelda hit the beach and unstrapped the leash from her ankle. Without drying off, she ran clumsily through the deep sand toward them, shouting. But

10

the ocean air seemed to snatch her words before they could reach the girls.

Piper cupped her hands to her mouth. "What?!"

"I found out"—*deep breath, deep breath*—"how to make sure we get the same first-period class." Zelda plopped into the sand, shaking her seaweed-streaked blonde hair. "The waves are *awesome* today!"

"But what about the rest of our classes?" Izzy said.

Zelda arched her eyebrow. Izzy knew this was her *seriously?* look. She'd watched her perfect it in the mirror a million times.

Izzy bit her lip.

"It's better than nothing," Zelda said. "Plus, at the middle school, your first-period class is also your homeroom. And if we're in the same homeroom, it means we'll get the same lunch and X-block and stuff like that." She flicked a piece of seaweed from her arm. "Why don't you just say thank you, Izzy?"

"It's great, Zelda." Piper's smile showed more teeth than usual. "We knew you'd think of something. How'd you make it happen?"

"When I told my dad how upset I was about the Sea Stars being split up, he called the school. He talked to Mr. Cantor—he's the tech ed teacher there. He and my dad used to work together at the university. Anyway, Mr. Cantor runs a class where the students do a news program called the *Shoreline Regional Middle School News*. My dad took me there and Mr. Cantor gave us a tour of the studio. You get a grade and everything. He's never let sixth graders do it before, but my dad says a bunch of kids quit at the last minute, so he needs students."

Izzy looked from Zelda to Piper and back. "What do you mean *do the news*?"

"We use real equipment like cameras and there's a green screen and computers and sound equipment, and we put the school news together and then report it."

"So, we'll be on TV?" Piper asked.

"Yeah—not TV you can see at home, but school TV," Zelda said. "Also, we won't be able to do music or art so your parents have to call the school to say it's okay."

"What do you mean we can't do art?" Izzy asked.

"Tech ed meets first period, same as the specials, so we can only take one or the other, but this is so much better, right?" Zelda leapt into a cartwheel, kicking up sand.

"Couldn't your dad get us into a different homeroom?" Izzy asked. When Zelda didn't answer right away, Izzy let her gaze fall to her feet, adding, "I'm sorry, Zelda, but you know art's my favorite and—"

"What have *you* done to keep us together, Izzy?" Zelda glared.

The thought of having to speak on television to a whole school full of strangers made the angry-ocean sound grow louder. "You know I can't talk in front of people, Zelda." Izzy dug her hand in her pocket, gripping her key.

Zelda rolled her eyes. "Can't or won't?"

Izzy wondered if there was a difference.

After an awkward pause, Piper asked, "But you're going to do it, right, Izzy?"

Izzy felt as if she was being backed into a corner. A mental image of her facing a giant news camera flashed across her brain. Her mouth went dry.

"If you don't do it, you'll end up stuck and alone in some random homeroom where you don't know anyone," Zelda said.

Piper nudged Izzy with her shoulder. "It's the only way to keep the Sea Stars together."

"You have to do it," Zelda said.

Izzy bit her lower lip.

As if sensing that Izzy was about to lose it, Piper thrust her arm out in front of her. "Sea Star triangle!" she shouted.

Izzy looked at her friend. While Zelda's crazy schemes often dragged her in over her head, Piper was the calm voice keeping her afloat. As she grabbed Piper's forearm below the elbow, she felt as if they were five years old all over again.

With a cold, dripping hand, Zelda grabbed hold of Izzy's arm and Piper grabbed Zelda's.

Their arms formed a triangle.

Zelda arched her eyebrow as her seaweed-green eyes took on a mischievous glint. "The Sea Stars are magic," she said. "We will be best friends forever."

Piper giggled as the girls raised their arms high, letting them slip apart—same as they had done a million times before.

Zelda cartwheeled off. "Make sure your parents call Mr. Cantor!" She ran toward her surfboard, re-attached the leash, and carried it into the ocean.

14

Izzy watched her paddle like mad against the breaking waves. Up and over . . . up and over, again.

Piper elbowed her. "It'll be great, Izzy. You know Zelda. It always works out."

A swell of water curled in a wave. Zelda popped up on her board, raising her hands in the air. The look on her face was pure joy.

As much as Izzy admired her friend, she was also jealous. Everything was easy for Zelda.

"She's not going to be able to keep us together forever," Izzy said.

"Can we get through sixth grade for now?" Piper smiled.

Izzy nodded, but she couldn't smile back.

Chapter 2

Izzy and Piper made their way back down the beach as Flotsam trotted next to them, carrying a clump of dried seaweed in his mouth.

"He always has to find something gross," Izzy said.

"Where's your bike?" Piper asked as they neared the beach parking lot.

"I took the skiff across the pond," Izzy said.

"You are so lucky!" Piper said. "I wish I could come over now, but, you know . . ."

"Tutor," Izzy finished with an exaggerated frown.

"Yeah. See you tomorrow." Piper took a few steps,

then paused and turned back. "Hey, Izzy, what did the ocean say to the shore?" she asked.

Izzy shrugged.

"Nothing. It just waved."

Izzy smiled as Piper disappeared into the parking lot. Then she headed back down the sandy path to the pond side of the barrier beach.

"Flotsam!" she called as she waded into the pond's mucky floor toward the skiff.

A rustling sound came from the bushes, and Flotsam popped out—galloping through the shallow water before leaping onto the skiff. He took his place on the bow, looking like a ship's figurehead.

Izzy climbed in after him, then hoisted the dripping anchor. She stored it under her seat, then pulled the cord to start the outboard motor. The engine sputtered. She yanked the cord again, giving the throttle a quick twist. As the motor sprang to life, she hit reverse, turning the boat around.

The only good part of moving to the marina was Oceanside Pond. Even though their old house on Rosewood Avenue was barely three miles away, her parents had never brought her to the pond until their move—instead choosing to spend their time at the beach or on her dad's commercial fishing boat, the *Isabella Rose*.

From the moment she'd showed up at the marina, the pond called to her to explore its hidden coves, oyster beds, and sunken barges.

Now Izzy took it all in as she puttered down the barrier coast, past its weathered row of cottages—pink and green and yellow and gray.

Seagulls and piping plovers soared above, occasionally dive-bombing the water in search of bait fish or a crab. Egrets filled the trees like Christmas ornaments and jellyfish floated serenely by.

When the sound of churning water grew loud, Izzy swung wide, careful to avoid the breachway—a man-made channel dug through the narrowest section of the barrier beach that connected the pond to the ocean. Lined with boulders, it was where the quiet pond met the rugged Atlantic in what Izzy thought looked like a witch's bubbling cauldron.

Izzy was terrified to get too close to the breachway, worried its unpredictable current would suck her and her tiny skiff inside its roiling waters and spit them into the Atlantic. She'd seen bigger boats fail to navigate the breachway, getting tossed against its rocks and sinking like toy boats in a bathtub.

After clearing the breachway, Izzy circled past Seagull Island until she reached the Seabury Oyster Farm. As she rounded Horseshoe Point, Oceanside Pond Marina came into view.

As vibrant as the pond was, the marina was decrepit. Although thirty slips were built into the five docks that stretched into its harbor, only ten were occupied with boats.

The main building, an old seafarer's mansion, rose out of the ground in three storm-gray stories. Izzy thought it must have looked majestic at one time. But now its shingles were warped and mildewed, and its sign was so faded it merely read OCE N SI E P ND M RI A.

Heavy black shutters dangled crookedly around yellowed windows. A large flat roof, which appeared to have at one time served as a balcony, maintained less than half of its spindled banister.

The bait and tackle shop on the first floor sold everything a boater could need, from handheld GPS devices to radar and outboard motors to fishing poles and lures. There was even a freezer full of squid.

Izzy lived in the second-floor apartment with her father and grandmother, Starenka, who'd moved in with them in May when Izzy's mom had left for Block Island. The dilapidated third-floor apartment was vacant, except for Mom's sewing machine and her other things waiting to be unpacked when she finally came home.

Almost a year ago, Izzy's dad had been deployed for the second time with the Rhode Island Army National Guard, to fight in the war in Afghanistan. He was supposed to be there for a year, but in January, they got word that there had been an explosion.

Izzy had hidden in her room as her mom waited by the phone for news. No matter how tightly Izzy covered her ears, she couldn't help but overhear words she'd never heard before, like *VBIED* and *PTSD*— and some she knew too well, like *convoy* and *detonate* and *critical condition*.

When Dad became well enough to be brought to a special hospital in Texas, Mom flew to see him. No matter how much Mom tried to prepare her, Izzy barely recognized her father when he finally came home in March.

It wasn't only the way he'd changed on the outside—like the way the right corner of his mouth wouldn't smile when the rest of his face did, and the way his right leg dragged when he got tired. Other things were different too. Dad wasn't able to manage small tasks like going to the mini-super for groceries, or big ones like operating his commercial fishing business, which he ended up having to put up for sale. To Izzy, it felt as if only a part of her dad had come home from Afghanistan and the best part—the Dad part—seemed to have gotten left behind.

When he first came home, Izzy would often find him up in the middle of the night, mumbling and pacing and making plans to reenlist. She wondered if it was because he needed to go back to find the parts he'd left behind. This terrified Izzy and sent her mom to her room in tears. Finally, he started seeing a therapist, and little by little, Izzy could see her dad coming home, for real. That was when he'd found the marina for sale.

"This is the answer," he had said when he brought them to see it.

But Mom didn't think living at a marina was an answer to anything, so when her aunts called to say that they were too old and too tired to keep running their family restaurant on Block Island, Mom was more than a little happy to move there for the summer to help keep Loretta's Kitchen afloat.

"I'll be home by Labor Day," she kept telling Izzy while she packed her suitcase. "You'll hardly know I'm gone," she said. "The summer will go by quicker than a flash of the North Light."

But Izzy had overheard Mom tell Dad a different story when she thought Izzy wasn't listening. "I think the time away will be good for both of us," she had said.

It hadn't made sense to Izzy that right when the rest of Dad was finally coming home, Mom decided to leave.

Izzy guided the skiff into the marina's harbor, immediately finding her father at the fuel dock, pumping gas for a sport fishing boat. She watched him hang the hose before walking the length of the dock to meet her at the skiff's slip.

She tossed him the bowline and he pulled the boat inside before securing the rope to its cleat. Flotsam leapt onto the dock and shook, spraying water everywhere.

Dad wiped his face with the back of his hand. "Thanks, Flotsam," he said. Then he turned toward Izzy. "How'd the mapping go?"

She cut the motor and hopped out to tie the stern line. Then she opened her patchwork bag, removing the maps. "I measured the pond side of Brogee's."

Her dad gave a soft whistle as he reviewed her work. "You've marked the height of each rock formation. I didn't know there were so many in there." He looked up at her. "Everyone's going to be a lot safer with this information."

"I'm going to use the soundings I collected to draw out each boulder." She pointed to a cluster of numbers. "They form kind of a semicircle pattern. Then, right here it gets deeper. My maps are going to be as detailed as Marie Tharp's."

"Marie Tharp, eh?" her father said with his half smile. "You sure love that book."

When they had moved into their apartment, her new bedroom was empty except for a bookshelf containing a dusty book titled *Soundings*. It told the story of Marie Tharp, the first scientist to map the ocean floor. Izzy devoured the story. It inspired her to make her own map of the pond.

"How's your sounding line holding up?"

Izzy held out the long knotted string. One end was attached to a piece of driftwood she used as a handle. The other was tied to one of her dad's five-ounce fishing weights. It was what she used to make the soundings—or measurements—of the pond.

"Still good," she said.

"Have you done around the breachway yet?"

Izzy looked at her feet. "I'm afraid of the breachway. I'm worried it will suck me into the Atlantic."

"You can do it, Iz. Just remember to stay in front of the current. If you're faster than it, then you're in control. If you're slower—then it's in control of you." He returned the papers to her with a wink. "Make sure to leave our secret clamming spots out of the final version."

Izzy smiled as she tucked her work back inside the bag. "Don't worry, Dad," she said.

"How much do you have left?"

"I'm not sure. I have to draw this out and add it to

the master. The pond's at least three miles long, and I've done less than a mile so far. With school starting, who knows?"

"Speaking of school," he said. "A teacher called. Mr. Cantor?" Her father grabbed the hose off its hook and began rinsing down the skiff. "He wanted my permission so you could do the school news. You didn't tell me about that."

The hose leaked and Izzy watched as water pooled around her feet. "What did you tell him?"

Flotsam started drinking from the puddle. Her father shifted the hose so he could drink fresh water instead.

"Dad, what did you say?"

"I said okay. You're all signed up."

The bag slipped from Izzy's shoulder. She caught it before it hit the ground. "Why'd you do that?"

Her dad shut off the water and began rolling up the hose. "I thought it's what you wanted. Mr. Cantor told me that Zelda and Piper are doing it."

"You should have asked me first."

Like a flip of a switch, her father's tone shifted. "I can't read minds, Isabella," he snapped. "Do it or don't do it, I don't care."

Izzy bit her lip.

Her father looked at his watch. "Why don't you call Mom before the restaurant gets busy?"

"Dad, today's Labor Day. We're picking her up at nine from the ferry."

Her father stared at the hose.

"Dad?" Izzy said.

He cleared his throat. "She called. She says the restaurant's still busy."

"Can't Uncle Pete bring her over later on his boat? She can't miss my first day of school, right?"

But her dad didn't answer. Instead he watched a Sea Hunter cruise down the dredged channel toward the marina.

"I need to take care of them." He headed back to the fuel dock. "Starenka's upstairs listening to the game," he called back. "She made stuffed cabbage for supper."

Izzy stuck her tongue out. The Sea Hunter tied up and two men began to lug a cooler onto the dock.

"Whatcha got there?" her dad called to them.

"Sea bass! Loads of 'em," one of them said as they carried it toward the cutting station.

Izzy watched her dad make his way toward the boat. She knew he was tired when she saw his right foot starting to drag. After working on an ocean-slicked deck with ease for his whole life, his steps were now wobbly and off-balance.

Suddenly, Izzy wanted her dad to call Mr. Cantor and tell him he'd made a mistake. She couldn't do the news after all.

Instead, she held her patchwork bag close to her heart, wishing the rest of the world could be more like her maps—predictable and safe.

Kindergarten

If you asked Zelda, she'd tell you that she invented the Sea Stars.

It was the first day of kindergarten and I didn't know anyone. Zelda says I was crying (I wasn't). She says Piper was hiccuping because she was scared. (That's probably true.)

So Zelda went to the art station and made special invitations. She pressed them into our hands like a secret.

Piper wiped her nose with the back of her hand as she stared at her note.

"What does it say?" I asked.

"You can't read?"

I felt my ears get hot.

Behind thick black glasses, Zelda's eyebrow arched. "Oh, for goodness' sake, come on!" She grabbed Piper and me by the sleeves and dragged us to the water table that Mrs. Robert had filled special with floating plastic sea animals for the first day of school.

"Look at all the starfish," Zelda said. She lifted a pink one and put it, dripping, onto the back of my hand.

"They aren't starfish," I said. "They're sea stars."

Zelda stared hard at me and I could see that her too-big eyeglasses had no lenses. With one finger, she pushed them tight against her face.

Piper sniffled.

I reached into the tank and put an orange sea star on Piper's hand. She sucked in her breath. Zelda found a purple one and we put our hands together so our plastic sea stars' tentacles could touch. I caught Piper smiling at me. I smiled back and thought maybe kindergarten wouldn't be so bad.

"Well, look at you," Mrs. Robert said, sweeping over in her flower-print dress. "You're like your own little group of sea stars." She put a finger to her lips. "I wonder what that's called?" she said. "I don't think it's a school like fish are in." She put her hands on her hips. "Well, you three will have to find out for me." And she marched off to make Roger stop licking his glue stick.

Zelda raised her sea star higher and in a funny SpongeBob voice said, "We are the Sea Stars."

Piper and I giggled.

Zelda grabbed hold of my arm below the elbow. "Now you hold my arm, Piper, and Izzy, you grab Piper's."

Our arms formed a triangle.

"The Sea Stars are magic," Zelda said. Her eyes were the color of dark seaweed and looked so serious inside those empty glasses that I knew what she was saying must be true. "We will be best friends forever."

Chapter 3

The next morning, Izzy rolled over in bed. The only good part about the first day of school was Mom's special breakfast. Izzy sniffed the air for the sweet scent of waffles, and listened for the sizzle of bacon.

But the only smell wafting through the apartment was diesel fumes from the boatyard, and the only sound was the boat crane, busy at work.

When Izzy had called her mom the night before, she'd gotten her voice mail. Now she checked her phone, but the one text wasn't from Mom.

Zelda: Hey Sea Star

Izzy: Hey

Zelda: Ready for our first day? 😊

Izzy: 👎 👎 👎

Flotsam scrambled into Izzy's room, tail thumping the bed, a tennis ball in his mouth.

"I know." Izzy tugged on the ball. "It feels like summer but we can't go on the pond." She frowned. "Believe me, I'm sadder than you."

Beep.

GM Sea Stars!

It was Piper texting in the Sea Star group chat. She'd be hurt to know Zelda hadn't included her in the last text, so Izzy moved to that one.

Piper: My mother is making me wear Bermuda shorts 😫

Zelda: At least u will pass fingertip test lol

Izzy couldn't help but smile at that. In fifth grade, the principal loved to make the girls put their arms by their sides to see if their shorts were "code length." If their fingertips went below their shorts, they had to wear a crunchy T-shirt that smelled like BO. When Zelda got coded for too-short shorts, she didn't flinch. Instead, she gathered the shirt at her waist with her hair elastic. Soon everyone else was wearing their T-shirts like Zelda.

Piper: Did you ask your mom about PTO stuff. I can bring it when we sleep over Saturday

Izzy: Not yet. GTG.

She tossed her phone on the bed.

Through her opened window, she could hear her father outside on his cell phone. "That's fantastic, Hassan," he was saying. "I'm glad you changed your mind. Izzy will be so excited . . ."

When she heard the name Hassan, she knew her dad was talking to his friend and former interpreter from Afghanistan. Dr. Haidary and his family had moved from Kabul to the United States and had resettled in Connecticut not long after her dad had come home in March. Although she'd never met them, she knew Dr. Haidary and his wife had a daughter and two young sons. She didn't understand why her name would come up in their conversation, but she didn't want to think about it either. Whenever Izzy heard her father begin to talk about Afghanistan is when she stopped listening.

"This is it, Flotsam." Izzy sighed. "No more hiding on the pond." She stared at the neat pile of clothes she'd laid out the night before, and instead dug through her drawers until she found the T-shirt she'd bought on the fifth-grade class trip to Block Island. On its front, a pink sea star wore sunglasses. A thought bubble over its head read WICKED COOL SUMMER. Zelda had picked it out so the three of them would have matching shirts. Izzy secretly hoped Piper and Zelda would wear theirs too.

She peeked into her patchwork bag and started to remove her maps, then decided to leave them in case she had a chance to work on them at school. She tossed in a new pencil and a notebook.

Ten minutes later, Izzy stood in the doorway to the kitchen staring at the empty table. Starenka sat in her chair, sipping black coffee and reading the *Providence Journal* sports section.

There were no waffles. No sizzling bacon. No Mom. Nothing but the hissing of the coffeepot and Starenka.

Her grandmother peered over her paper. She wore a gray sweater over her cotton-print dress, even though it was already sweltering in the apartment. Her long silver hair was braided and secured in a tight bun at the back of her head.

"Pod' sem," Starenka said. "What do you say to your old babička?"

"Dobré ráno," Izzy said as she leaned in to give her grandmother a hug.

Starenka's family had come to the United States as immigrants. Even though Starenka was born in Pennsylvania, she didn't understand English until she started school and loved to speak to Izzy in her first language, Slovak.

Starenka gave her a soggy kiss on the cheek. Izzy could tell she hadn't put her teeth in yet.

"That's for good luck on the first day of school."

"Thanks, Starenka. Where's Mom?"

"Ack." Starenka waved her hand as if she was shooing a fly. Then she returned to her black coffee and paper.

Izzy decided to drop the subject. She didn't want to aggravate Starenka, who was just as upset as Izzy was about Mom's decision to spend the summer on Block Island. She opened the cupboard and dug out last year's lunch bag. She peeked inside, giving it a sniff, and immediately wished she'd thought to wash it out last night.

"How'd you do yesterday?" Izzy asked as she dropped a Pop-Tart into the toaster.

Starenka immediately cheered up. "Yankees won again." She gave a toothless grin. "Tony Macaroni's gonna owe me money!"

Izzy couldn't help but smile back. Her grandmother loved to place bets with her bookie, Tony Macaroni, as she called him. Izzy had never met Tony, but she heard all about him whenever Starenka won big.

"Where's Dad?"

"Working, working," she said. "My son is the hardest worker."

Izzy frowned. Dad had never been one to sit still, but since Afghanistan, his perpetual motion was nervous and restless. Izzy was eating her Pop-Tart and packing her lunch when the apartment door opened.

Before she could turn, her father lifted her off the

ground in a bear hug, spinning her until she felt dizzy. His shirt was thick with the smell of sea salt and engine grease.

"Middle school," he said. "I can't believe it." His mouth curved in its half smile.

Izzy slipped out of his grasp.

"So, Mom couldn't make it," she said, doing her best to keep her voice flat.

Dad cleared his throat. "It was too foggy last night for Pete to take the boat across."

Izzy opened a cupboard, pretending to search for the Marshmallow Fluff. She hated that something as silly as waffles could make her cry. With the back of her hand, she swiped away a tear.

When she turned around, she caught her dad staring. "What?" she asked.

"You look taller today. That's all." He frowned. "I forgot to measure you last night."

Each year, on the night before the first day of school, Dad had Izzy stand against her bedroom door frame and marked how tall she was. But that was before the move. Somehow Izzy felt that she'd be betraying their old cottage if they restarted their tradition at the marina.

She opened the Fluff and spread it across a piece of bread.

Her father slapped his hand against his forehead. "What was I thinking?" he said. "I was supposed to make a special back-to-school breakfast. Where's the waffle iron?" He began rummaging through a cupboard.

"It's not in there," Izzy said. "It doesn't matter. I already ate."

"When I was eleven years old, I was milking cows before school," Starenka said with an emphatic nod. "No one makes waffles for me."

"Oh, Ma," Dad said. "Times have changed."

"Ack." With a snap of the paper, Starenka returned to her sports section.

Dad grabbed the coffeepot, which dripped on the floor as he poured his cup. "Are you excited, Iz? Middle school." He shook his head.

Izzy swallowed hard.

"You'll meet so many new friends." He took a sip.

"I already have friends; remember Zelda and Piper? I don't need any more." Izzy grabbed some grapes from the fridge. One rolled on the ground and Flotsam jumped on it as if it were prey. Izzy scooped it up before he could eat it.

"You can never have too many friends."

The angry-ocean sound began to churn in Izzy's ears, making her feel heavy and dizzy at the same time. She swallowed hard. "So you talked to Mom last night?"

"Yup."

"And she'll be here for dinner tonight, right? She's not going to miss the entire first day of school."

Her father opened his mouth as if he was going to say something, then closed it.

"What?"

"There might be . . . well . . . I have a surprise for you tonight."

Izzy spun around. "Really? What is it?"

Dad gave his half smile. "If I told you, then it wouldn't be a surprise."

Izzy bit her lip, trying to contain her growing excitement. *Mom must be moving back home today after all!* Her body immediately felt lighter. She ran over and hugged her dad. "See you this afternoon," she said. She gave her grandmother a big kiss. "I love you, Starenka."

Her grandmother patted her cheek. "Good girl," she said.

Flotsam started to follow Izzy, but Dad crouched to hold him back. "Sorry, pup. You're stuck with me today."

Flotsam whined.

Izzy looked at her dad, kneeling on the floor. He had always been giant to her in every way, but since Afghanistan he seemed smaller. *The surgeries took a lot out of him*, her mom had reminded her. But Mom wasn't there to tell her everything would be okay anymore. Afghanistan messed that up too.

"I love you, Izzy-bug," Dad said. "Go tear it up at middle school, okay?"

Izzy swallowed hard. "Love you, too, Dad." The screen door slammed behind her as she raced for the bus.

The ride to school was quiet. As the bus wound its way down Carpenter Drive and around Surfside Avenue, Izzy put in her earbuds. She rested her forehead against the window, watching the cottages drift by. Most of the houses were empty now—summer people packed and gone for the season. She was so lost in thought that she didn't realize where she was until the scent of honeysuckle found her. She popped up in her seat, inhaling. Searching.

There it was: 55 Rosewood Avenue. She could almost pretend the light blue cottage with its sun-yellow front door was exactly the same as when they'd lived there only a few months ago. She could still make out the white curtains that floated in and out with the ocean breeze, and the SAVE THE NARWHALS sticker in her up-stairs bedroom window. But the SOLD sign piercing its front lawn made it clear that it wasn't the same at all.

Still, if she closed her eyes, she could convince her-self that if she walked inside, everything would be the same as it always had been. Dad would be at the table charting an offshore trip. Mom would be at the counter trying out a new recipe, Flotsam asleep at her feet.

More kids got on, and the doors folded shut behind them. The bus chugged forward, leaving the cottage in its exhaust.

Izzy fell back in her seat. She dug out the key and turned it over in her palm, rubbing its worn spots be-fore tucking it away. Like her maps, it was something that didn't change. Her parents hadn't seen her snag it when they turned the house keys over to the new owners. Somehow, saving that key was like holding on to a way home.

As the bus merged onto Route One, she felt a knee jam into her seat. She turned her music louder. The knee jammed again.

She didn't have to look to know Roger and Apollo were behind her. She ducked lower.

"Hey," Roger said, leaning over the back of her seat. Long, dark bangs fell across his eyes. "Skip says the new owners are going to tear your house down."

Skip was what everyone called Roger's dad—including Roger. He had worked for the previous owner of Oceanside Pond Marina until it went bankrupt. When Izzy's dad bought it from the bank, he somehow inherited Skip too.

"Cool!" said Apollo, flipping his shoulder-length, blond, wavy hair. "I want to see that."

Izzy ignored them.

"Tourists," Roger scoffed. "Beach house isn't good enough. Gotta build their McMansions." He shifted his weight, tugging harder on her seat.

Izzy frowned.

"Skip says your dad's in over his head at the marina." Roger laughed. "He says your dad doesn't know a Sunfish from a Bertram. He says that if it weren't for him, the marina'd go belly up, same as it did on the last owners."

Izzy spun around. "My dad's been a commercial fisherman for fifteen years. Running a marina is easy compared to that. It's not his fault that the place is in worse shape than the bank told him when he bought it."

Even beneath his overgrown bangs, Izzy could see Roger's eyes narrow. "Runnin' a fishing boat ain't nothin' like runnin' a marina. Skip's worked marinas his whole life."

"Well, why doesn't Skip go work somewhere else?"

Roger laughed again. "What would your old man do?"

Izzy spun away, ducking even lower in her seat. *Roger doesn't know what he's talking about*, she thought. But his words had churned up an uneasy feeling. She dug inside her pocket, holding the key tight in her fist.

As the bus pulled up to Shoreline Regional Middle, Izzy closed her eyes. School hadn't even started yet, and she was ready to go home.

Chapter 4

As they waited for the doors to open, Izzy scanned her new school. The building was at least three times larger than Seabury Elementary. Her stomach clenched as she watched kids standing in tight huddles outside the main entrance. She searched the crowd for Zelda or Piper or any familiar face, but she couldn't seem to find anyone she knew. For a moment she wondered if she'd been brought to the wrong place.

Finally, the bell rang and the doors opened. Izzy grabbed her patchwork bag and hunched her shoulders, making herself as small as possible. She followed the line of kids streaming into the school.

When she got near the front door, she heard someone yell, "Izzy!"

She turned to see Piper, wearing last year's lacrosse championship T-shirt with her Bermuda shorts.

Izzy was so relieved, she wanted to throw her arms around her friend, but she knew that would look stupid, so instead she just said, "Hey."

Zelda popped up next to them, wearing white jean shorts with rips in them, a black tank top, and sandals. "What's up, girls?" she said as she sipped from a Coffee Cabinet cup.

"My mother wouldn't let me wear my flip-flops," Piper said, staring at her socks and sneakers. "My feet are already sad."

"Nice shorts." Zelda grinned at Piper's Bermudas. "I think my grandmother has a pair like that."

Piper swatted her arm, but laughed anyway.

"My mom says that Rhode Island is the Bermuda of New England—or maybe it's Block Island. Anyway, I think you look good," Izzy said.

"Yeah," Piper said. "That's me. Miss Rhode Island."

Zelda arched her eyebrow. "I can't believe you're still wearing that shirt, Izzy. My mom uses mine to dust."

Izzy stared down at her pink sea star T-shirt. Suddenly, it seemed babyish compared to what Zelda and Piper were wearing.

"Let's go," Zelda said. "I want to show you guys the TV studio."

They followed Zelda, maneuvering down bright red locker-lined halls. Izzy kept as close to her friends as possible. Kids rushed in every direction, fist-bumping and high-fiving. It seemed as if everyone else knew each other. The angry-ocean sound grew.

"Here's my locker," Zelda said.

"Mine's next door!" Piper grinned.

Izzy frowned. Already separated. She continued down the hall until she found number 876. She spun the combination like she had practiced: right, left, right. She pulled. Nothing.

She spun again, careful to pause at each number. Nothing.

The first bell rang. "Come on, Izzy," Piper said as she

and Zelda made their way to a door marked TECHNOLOGY EDUCATION.

Izzy gave up and heaved her bag onto her shoulder.

Inside the tech ed room, Izzy blinked. The back wall was painted lime green. In front of it sat a table and chairs that faced two large, black television cameras. Across the studio, there was an enclosed room with a long, wide window stretching across it. Izzy could easily see inside the windowed room, where a tall, gray-haired man leaned over a boy and girl wearing headphones.

The girl pointed at them through the window and the man removed the headphones and stepped into the studio. "Welcome," he said. "I am Mr. Cantor." He was wearing a gray business suit with a purple polka-dot bow tie. He reminded Izzy of an olden-day news reporter.

"You must be Miss Grenier and Miss Mancini," Mr. Cantor said. "Miss Akins told me all about you. Are you ready to learn about the television news profession?"

Izzy jammed her hand into her pocket, gripping the key so tightly that it dug into her palm.

"I'm sure Miss Akins has explained to you that this is a highly selective class. The equipment is expensive." He removed a red handkerchief from his pocket and coughed into it. "And I usually don't allow sixth graders to participate, but . . . well, there was a need."

Izzy wondered if the need was that everyone had quit because they were terrified of this guy.

"We will meet here for homeroom and first period, and will share the duties of a newsroom," he said. "You are to arrive on time. I do not excuse tardies." He fixed his gaze sharply on them. "I take this class very seriously. To succeed, you will have to learn each facet of the television news business and master each one."

"What are . . . the, um . . . facets we have to learn?" Piper asked. Izzy noticed a catch in her voice.

Mr. Cantor's mouth curved in what might have been a smile, but looked more like the face a shark makes before it eats its prey. "I'll let Miss Akins give you the tour."

Izzy glanced around the studio with its bright lights and complicated equipment. She longed for her fifth-grade classroom, where the day began with quiet reading.

"I'm looking for Mr. Cantor," someone said.

All heads turned toward the doorway.

"I . . . um . . . I think I'm in this class," Roger said.

Izzy shook her head. The day couldn't get any worse.

"Ah! Mr. Johnson, I presume," Mr. Cantor said.

Roger dug his hands into his jeans pockets.

Mr. Cantor turned toward Zelda. "I believe everyone's here now. Miss Akins, are you ready to proceed with the tour?"

"Yup," Zelda said.

Mr. Cantor peered at her over his wire-rimmed glasses.

"Um, I mean, yes, sir," she corrected herself.

"Perfect." Mr. Cantor's shoes made a sharp clicking sound as he made his way back inside the windowed room.

When he was out of earshot, Piper whispered, "Zelda! What have you gotten us into?"

Zelda waved away her question, then marched toward a computer set on a desk to the left of the anchor table. "As Mr. Cantor said," she began, "this is where we write the script. Whatever we type here"—she hopped over to a screen near the cameras—"will show up here." She stood next to the teleprompter, where SEA STARS RULE THE WORLD flashed across the screen.

"That is pretty cool," Piper said.

Roger crossed his arms. "Why are there two cameras?"

"Camera B is broken, so I don't know, but check this out." Zelda stood behind camera A. "Piper, go sit at the anchor table."

Piper ran around the table and slid into a chair.

"This button lets you zoom in and out on the person at the desk," Zelda said. "See?" Piper's face filled the TV screen, then got smaller again.

"Come on," she said as she led them to the windowed room. "Next is the control room—where the sound, graphics, and editing are done." Inside, Mr. Cantor adjusted a screen while two students looked on. Everyone was wearing headphones.

The girl closest to them removed her headphones and spun to face them. She wore a short dress and sparkly eye makeup. Izzy thought she looked like a high school student. She crossed her arms to cover her sea star T-shirt.

"Hi, I'm Taylor." She pointed to the boy. "Nathaniel and I were just picking the closing music for the broadcast. What do you think? I say 'Shake It Off' and Nathaniel wants some band no one knows."

Mr. Cantor removed his headphones. "I am quite familiar with Pink Floyd," he said. "We will not be playing a song that contains the lyrics, 'we don't need no education' on the first day of school, Mr. Richards."

Taylor shot a fist in the air. "Score one for the Taylors," she said.

"You have a lot to learn about music," Nathaniel said.

"I like Pink Floyd," Roger said.

"Now that we are all together, please meet my resident experts—Miss Allen and Mr. Richards are both eighth graders." He beamed at them. "They were the *only* students last year to have earned my trust, so I have given them great creative leeway. Something you should all strive for."

Izzy swallowed hard. She couldn't believe she was missing art for this.

Mr. Cantor continued. "After the news is recorded, the feed comes in here. One or two of you will be on sound—and same for graphics. When you receive the feed, you will edit accordingly. Everything must be complete by the end of first period when I send it out to all the classrooms. You will be able to watch the final version during your second-period class."

Izzy's head began to ache.

"Since it is the first day of school," Mr. Cantor said, "I have already prepared today's script, but I'd like each of you to develop your own personal screen presence. After you read the requisite teacher announcements, the lunch menu, and a spot I call 'This Day in History,' I'd like you to personalize your report. Put your own signature on it, so to speak."

"But w-we . . . we aren't doing the news today, are we?" Izzy said.

Mr. Cantor shot her a look that made her want to melt into the ground. He pointed at a whiteboard hung next to the computer desk. "Each morning, I will post your assignments. You need to check it when you arrive."

"Testing one, two, three . . ." Nathaniel spoke into a microphone. "Mr. Cantor, it's not working."

"I suggest everyone get started." Mr. Cantor put his headphones back on.

"Let's go," Zelda said.

The three of them followed her out.

Izzy scanned the whiteboard. She breathed a sigh of relief when she saw: SCRIPT: MANCINI. Zelda and Piper were anchors; Roger was manning the camera; Taylor and Nathaniel were on sound and graphics.

Izzy slipped into the seat at the computer desk before anything changed.

"I have an idea," Zelda said. "What if we do, like, an ocean fact or something to end the news? It could be our . . . you know, signature . . . like Mr. Cantor said."

"Okay," Piper said. "Izzy, you know all that science stuff."

Izzy swallowed hard. "Well," she said. "I know a lot of sea star facts." She started typing.

"*Eeek!*" Zelda squeaked. "That's so perf!"

Taylor walked over. "Are you guys all set? Let me know if you have any questions."

Piper glanced at the control room, where Mr. Cantor was still busy with Nathaniel. "Is he always so strict?" she whispered.

Taylor nodded with a grin. "Yeah, but if you're interested in TV production, there is no one better than Mr. Cantor. He worked at CNN when it was just starting. He knows everything about the news. We're lucky he wants to teach here."

"So what *really* happened to all the seventh and eighth graders?" Piper asked.

Taylor glanced at the control room and then back at the girls. "He failed them," she said. "It was really bad. That's why he's willing to let sixth graders in this class this year. Once everyone heard what happened, no one would sign up."

"Why did he do that?" Piper asked, her face turning a shade paler.

Taylor shrugged. "Like I said. Mr. Cantor takes the news seriously." She looked hard at the girls. "Don't worry. If you do what he says, you'll be fine."

54

Izzy waited for Zelda to apologize for dragging them into this. Instead she narrowed her eyes as if she was ready for the challenge.

Taylor turned toward Roger. "So, you're on camera today?"

Roger stood next to camera A as if he was guarding it. "Sure." He flipped his bangs out of his face. "I can do that."

Since the script was done, Izzy didn't know where to go. Suddenly, she worried Mr. Cantor would give her something else to do. She hugged her stomach and hunched forward, making herself as small as possible.

Mr. Cantor stepped out of the control room. "When we begin, I will count out loud: five, four, et cetera. Then I will silently count off the rest on my fingers so the mics don't pick up my voice." He pointed at Roger. "At the signal, you flip the switch and the camera light will turn green. That means we are live and recording. I expect absolute silence!"

Roger nodded.

"Okay, everyone ready?" He held up his hand.

"Five, four—" He lowered his fingers, one at a time, *three, two, one*. He pointed at Roger.

The camera light blinked green.

Zelda's face turned serious as the script began to scroll through the teleprompter. "Good morning. Today is Tuesday, September fourth, and this is your Shoreline Regional Middle School news," she said.

Izzy thought she heard a catch in her voice, but Zelda took a breath and continued. "Today is National Macadamia Nut Day."

"Lunch is turkey club sandwich," Piper said.

Zelda's forehead wrinkled. Izzy could tell she was trying to look serious.

"There will be an activities fair after school tomorrow," Piper reported. "Please stop by to learn about the many sports and clubs that Shoreline Regional Middle School has to offer."

"On this day in history, in 1888," Zelda continued, "the Kodak printing company was founded by George Eastman, who invented the first roll-film camera. Eastman's cameras made the hobby of photography accessible to everyone."

"Finally," Piper said, "we want to leave you with the science question of the day. When a sea star loses a limb, it is able to grow one back. How do scientists classify these animals that have the amazing ability to regenerate?"

"Tune in next time for the answer." As "Shake It Off" started to play, Zelda flashed a big smile. "This is Zelda Akins," she said.

"And Piper Grenier."

"Signing off!" they sang together. "See you tomorrow for more Shoreline Regional Middle School news."

Mr. Cantor motioned to Roger, who flipped the switch. When the light went dark, Zelda and Piper unhooked their microphones.

"That was awesome!" Zelda said.

Piper beamed.

Mr. Cantor was already retreating to the control room. "We only have forty minutes. Let's start editing!" he said.

Taylor came out to high-five Zelda and Piper. "Nice job!" she said.

Izzy watched the three girls huddled together. She uncrossed her arms, then crossed them again, not sure whether to stay put or join them as they made their way into the control room.

"That was pretty cool," Roger said.

Izzy stared at him. "How did *you* get into this class?"

Roger shrugged. "I didn't know I was doing it until this morning. Mrs. Cook, the principal, told me that Mr. Cantor needed more students."

Izzy stood. "I'm going into the control room."

Roger followed her.

Inside, everyone was watching Zelda and Piper on the screen. Taylor had changed the background to make it look as if they were reporting from the Eiffel Tower. Everyone was laughing, even Mr. Cantor.

"Roger, want to help me with sound?" Nathaniel asked.

It seemed as if everyone had a job but Izzy. She shifted her feet, wanting to leave but not knowing where to go. She looked at the clock. There was still a half hour left. As all the girls except Izzy put on a set of headphones, a new question popped into her head: *If the Sea Stars lost a limb, would they regenerate too?*

First Grade

In first grade, Zelda saved my life.

In the school bathroom.

It sounds stupid, but it's true.

I was scared to go in there because of the words.

There were ugly words etched in big bold Sharpie and scratched into the dull green stalls.

Angry words written in deep gashes.

Sad words crossed out and repeated over and over.

Words about how Janis hated Masie and how Melanie thought Alex was a dingus (which must have been bad even though I didn't know what a dingus was).

It didn't matter that the words weren't about me. Or that they were probably written by fifth graders who I didn't even know. I did know that whoever wrote them wanted to hurt Masie and Alex.

No matter how bad I had to pee when I got to the bathroom, every time I saw those words, I was too scared to go anymore.

Even when Mrs. Howard marched me into a stall and waited outside, the angry words stared back at me. So I closed my eyes and crossed my legs. Tight.

But the problem was, I could only hold it for so long.

Recess was okay because I could run and move and keep things from coming out. Even in class, I could at least get up to use the pencil sharpener or grab a tissue.

But when we moved to the carpet for Read-Aloud, everyone had to sit real still and listen.

When Mrs. Howard read the part in Officer Buckle *where he falls off the swivel chair, the whole class burst out laughing. Including me. And, well, you can guess what happened.*

Zelda reacted first. She was sitting next to me. She saw my face. She immediately took off her sweater and raised her hand.

"Mrs. Howard?" she said. "I don't feel good. I think I'm going to puke."

Mrs. Howard's forehead wrinkled. "You were fine a minute ago, Zelda."

Zelda made gagging sounds. "Can Izzy come with me to the nurse? I'm going to lose my lunch."

Mrs. Howard's gaze moved from Zelda to me. I stared down at Zelda's sweater, now covering my lap. My ears felt as if they were on fire.

Mrs. Howard nodded. "Go ahead, girls."

Zelda helped me up, pulling her sweater tight around my waist as I stood. It was big and fluffy and covered everything to my knees.

She dragged me out of the classroom, making gagging sounds the whole way.

In the hallway I started to cry.

Zelda brought me into the bathroom, then pushed me into a stall.

The ugly words glared at me as I sat on the toilet.

"Zelda," I said. "I don't like this place."

"It's a bathroom, Izzy."

"The angry words make my stomach hurt."

I had never told anyone about how the bathroom words scared me. Even then I knew it sounded dumb.

Zelda gave a huge sigh, and although I couldn't see her, I knew she was probably practicing making her left eyebrow arch.

"They're just words, Izzy. They can't hurt you."

"Promise?" I said.

61

"Go, Izzy."

I went.

When I finished, I opened the door. Zelda had removed the leggings she'd been wearing beneath her jean skirt.

"Take off your pants and put these on," she said.

I went back into the stall and changed.

We wrapped my wet clothes in paper towels.

"Now tie my sweater around your waist again."

I looked at myself in the mirror. I felt warm and dry.

"All fixed," said Zelda.

I turned to her. "You are my best friend," I said.

"I know," she said.

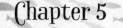

Chapter 5

Izzy spent most of the day counting the minutes until school was over. She was happy that Piper was in her language arts class and Zelda was in science.

She was relieved when Roger and Apollo weren't on the afternoon bus. And even happier that Flotsam was waiting for her in the boatyard when she got home. When he jumped up, Izzy took his paws in her hands and danced with him. "I missed you so much," she said.

She let Flotsam down and headed into the shop. "Dad!" she called as the screen door slammed shut behind her. But there was only Skip at the counter, picking through a pile of lures.

"Your old man's out on the docks," he said. The cigarette clenched in his teeth bobbed up and down with each word. "He just got a shipment of bugs."

"You're not supposed to smoke in here."

Skip pulled the cigarette from his mouth. "Got three bosses now, do I?" He held it up. "It's not lit." He returned his attention to the lures. "Can't believe I gotta work for some foreigner . . . too many bosses," he grumbled.

Izzy shook her head as she headed back outside. *What is he talking about?*

She found her dad at the cutting station. He was peering into a large white cooler. When he saw Izzy, he held up a lobster. It waved its banded claws at her.

When she was close, Dad said, "Not bad, huh? Bob brought these over from Point Jude. Special occasion— thought we'd have bugs for dinner."

Izzy grinned. Mom loved lobster.

"How was school?" he asked.

"Okay. So, I'm ready for my surprise!" Her voice squeaked with excitement. Finally having Mom home would make up for all the bad stuff that had happened that day.

"We have company," Dad said mysteriously as he headed toward the shop.

Mom's not company, Izzy thought as she followed him inside. The screen door slammed shut behind them.

"These lures are a mess," Skip said as they walked past him toward the stairs that led to the apartment.

"Thanks for getting them sorted out," Dad said.

Skip grunted.

Flotsam trotted behind them as they headed upstairs. When they got to the second floor, Izzy reached for the doorknob.

"One more flight," Dad said.

Oh, right, Izzy thought. Mom was probably getting all her stuff she'd stored on the third floor so she could finally put it away.

At the top of the stairs, Dad knocked.

The door opened and a tall man with thick black hair and a dark beard towered in front of them. "Salam alaykom," the man said. Behind him stood a girl holding a plastic pitcher. Even though it felt like a hundred degrees in the stuffy apartment, she wore a long-sleeved shirt with gold embroidery on the sleeves and jeans. A deep blue scarf covered her head and draped across her neck and shoulders so that only her face showed.

"Who are you?" Izzy snapped.

The girl started to take a step back but lost her footing. The pitcher slipped from her hand and ice water began to pool around her gold sandals. Her large brown eyes remained fixed on Izzy.

A woman appeared from the next room. She wore a long, gray embroidered dress that came down past her knees. Slits on the sides revealed loose tan pants. Like the girl, she wore a scarf around her head.

The woman said something to the girl in a language Izzy had never heard and they both fell to the ground, trying to scoop up the ice. The excitement was too much for Flotsam, who barreled into the apartment, barking and chasing ice cubes.

"No, Flotsam!" her father shouted.

Two young boys, probably around seven or eight, appeared. They covered their mouths, trying to hold back laughter as Flotsam skidded across the linoleum floor. Izzy's dad grabbed their dog by the collar and shepherded him outside.

Izzy followed them down the stairs. "Dad, what's going on? Where's Mom?"

After he put Flotsam outside, her father headed back up the stairs.

"Mom?" he asked.

Izzy had to take two steps at a time to keep up. "The surprise. That Mom's finally moving home."

"What are you talking about, Izzy? I never said Mom was coming home." He knocked on the door a second time. The bearded man appeared again.

"I'm so sorry, Hassan," her father began.

Hassan? Izzy realized the man was her father's army interpreter from Afghanistan—the person she had overheard him talking to that morning.

"There is nothing to be sorry for, my friend," the man said. The corners of his eyes creased deeply, as though they were smiling. "Please come in and make yourself comfortable." He guided them past the girl and her mother, who were at the sink.

The third-floor apartment was identical to the one below. Izzy followed her father into what would be their TV room downstairs. But this room had no television or furniture. Instead, bulging suitcases and

67

boxes were stacked against one wall. A rickety fan sat in the corner, barely sputtering out a breeze. A red carpet with intricate designs sewn into it was spread across the floor. Large, flat cushions, covered in dark red fabric, encircled the room.

Izzy hugged herself.

"I apologize for my daughter," the man said. "It has been a difficult week, and we are all a little—how do you say—jumpy."

"I think we're the ones who should be apologizing, Hassan," Izzy's father said as he nudged Izzy.

She studied her father's face. *Does he want me to say I'm sorry?*

Her dad placed his hand on Dr. Haidary's shoulder. "Izzy," he said. "This is the man who saved my life."

Izzy wanted to cover her ears. Since her father had come home from Afghanistan, she had refused to listen to his stories about what he'd experienced— especially the story about how he almost died there. She sure wasn't going to listen to it now.

"You exaggerate, my friend," Dr. Haidary said. "But I am pleased to finally meet you, zmâ lur."

The woman came into the room and stood next to

her husband. She wrung her hands, staring at them instead of Izzy or her father.

"Please meet my wife, Meena," Dr. Haidary said to Izzy.

Mrs. Haidary gave a quick smile. "Salam alaykom."

"Welcome!" Izzy's dad replied. "I'm so happy to finally meet you in person."

The boys returned and tugged on their father's sleeve.

"And these are our sons, Hikmat and Ali."

The older boy leaned in to whisper to his father.

"They are asking about the dog," Dr. Haidary said.

"Flotsam's outside," Dad said. "He'd love it if the boys would like to play catch."

Dr. Haidary nodded at the boys, who scrambled toward the door. Mrs. Haidary called after them in their language.

"She wants to be sure they stay far from the water."

Izzy heard the door slam and the boys' footsteps tumble down the stairs.

The girl returned with a tray of glasses filled with ice water. She gave a shy smile as she handed a glass to Izzy.

"This is my daughter, Sitara," Dr. Haidary said to Izzy. "I believe you are the same age. Eleven?"

Izzy nodded.

Dr. Haidary pointed at the cushions. "Please have a seat on the toshak. Make yourself comfortable."

Izzy sat next to her father. She kept her gaze focused on the floor. Sitara knelt next to her.

Why are they here? Are they going to be living here? Izzy wanted to ask. *For how long? And where are Mom's things?* She shook her head. *Mom is not going to like this one bit.*

Izzy's mother had wanted her dad to put Afghanistan, and all the bad stuff it caused, behind them. *How can he forget about Afghanistan if Afghanistan has moved in upstairs?*

"Izzy . . . ?" Dad said.

Everyone was looking at her.

"Dr. Haidary asked you what grade you're in."

"Um . . . sixth."

"This is perfect news," Dr. Haidary said. "Sitara will be in your class."

Izzy glanced at Sitara, who was still staring at her with her large, unblinking brown eyes.

"We change classes and it's hard to get in the same ones," Izzy said. "It's a regional school and there are a lot more kids."

"Yes," Dad said. "But I called about that TV news class you're doing with Zelda and Piper. Mr. Cantor said Sitara can join too. Why don't you tell her what it's like?"

Izzy looked around at the strange faces staring at her. Suddenly, she felt as if she'd traveled to some foreign place. Nothing was familiar—not their language or clothes or these cushions they were sitting on.

"Izzy?" her father repeated.

Her stomach sank as she thought about Mr. Cantor and his purple polka dots and his rules. "I don't know. Kids do the news." She wanted to add that the teacher was really mean, too, but she figured that would get another look from her dad.

The faces kept staring.

"And . . . ," her father said.

"And that's it. My best friends, Piper and Zelda, were the anchors today, while I pretty much did nothing."

The angry-ocean sound was starting in Izzy's ears. She felt as if she were suffocating. *I need to get out of this apartment*, she thought. *Now!* "I'm going to check on Flotsam," she said.

Without waiting for permission, she scrambled through the kitchen and ran down the stairs. Outside, she breathed deeply, letting the ocean breeze cool her. A gull cawed and water splashed as a boater rinsed down his Grady-White.

Neither Flotsam nor the boys were anywhere to be seen. Izzy crossed the chipped stone yard, ducking around boats set on wood blocks that were waiting for repairs. She thought about what Roger had said on the bus: *Skip says that if it weren't for him, the marina'd go belly up again . . .*

She knew that the owners would only wait so long for their boats to be fixed before taking them somewhere else. Fishing was at its best in September.

She dug her hand in her pocket until she found the key. Her pounding heart seemed to slow with it tight in her fist.

Finally, at the far corner of the boatyard, Izzy found the boys throwing a stick for Flotsam to retrieve. Each time he dropped it at their feet, the boys squealed in delight.

"Flotsam!" Izzy called.

But Flotsam ignored her, instead barking for Hikmat to throw the stick again.

Izzy crossed her arms as she approached them.

"This dog has an unusual name," Hikmat said.

Izzy studied the boys. They acted much older than they looked. "You speak English really well," she said.

"Our father taught us. He was a medical doctor in Afghanistan," Ali said.

"But then he became an interpreter for the US Army," Hikmat added. "Plus we've been living in Connecticut for five months already. We're all very good at English now."

"Except Mor," Ali said. "That's what we call our mother. She doesn't understand."

"What language do you speak?" Izzy asked.

"We speak Pashto at home—but we know Dari too," Ali said.

"There are many languages spoken in Afghanistan," added Hikmat.

"You already know three languages?" Izzy said.

"Of course," Hikmat answered.

Flotsam rolled onto his back and Ali knelt down to rub his belly. Flotsam seemed to give Izzy a look as if to say, *I could get used to this.*

"What kind of dog is he?" Hikmat asked.

"We're not sure. My dad says he's probably a mix of border collie and black Lab."

"What does his name mean?" Ali asked.

"Flotsam is what they call the stuff that falls off ships and barges that washes up onshore," Izzy said. "When we lived on Rosewood Avenue, Flotsam showed up in our yard looking like he'd just fallen off a boat. His fur was wet and matted." Izzy knelt and began scratching Flotsam behind the ear. "He'd knocked over our garbage can and was eating out of it."

She smiled, thinking back to that day. Mom helped give him a bath and they nailed FOUND signs around town. Dad told Izzy not to get attached, but after a month, when no one came for him, Dad said Flotsam could stay as long as he wanted.

Ali turned to his brother. "I told you this place would be great. Puppies wash up from the ocean."

Hikmat rolled his eyes.

Izzy frowned. "It only happened once."

"Ali! Hikmat!" Dr. Haidary called.

"Thank you for letting us play with Flotsam," Hikmat said. The boys ran toward their father. Flotsam started to follow them, but Izzy called him back.

"Stay," she said sternly. "You're supposed to be *my* friend, remember?"

Flotsam gave her a goofy grin. She thought he looked sorry.

Izzy's dad was setting up lobster pots on propane burners. Mrs. Haidary and Sitara each gripped a handle from the cooler and carried it toward him.

Starenka sat at the picnic table, shucking corn. Mrs. Haidary and Sitara moved there to help her.

Dad walked over to Izzy.

She jammed her hands in her pockets.

"That was rude running out like that," he said.

Izzy's mouth fell open. *Rude?* She wanted to point out that forgetting to make a special back-to-school breakfast was rude. And Mom missing her first day of school was rude.

Instead she swallowed hard. Her throat felt scratchy and tight.

"I thought Mom was the surprise you told me about this morning. I thought she was finally moving home."

"Mom?" Dad sighed. "I told you she was staying on for another week at the restaurant."

"A week? You never told me a week!"

"She wants you to come to the island on Saturday and—"

"She's totally missing the first day of school?" Izzy blinked hard.

"You can celebrate together on Saturday when you—"

"I don't want to celebrate the first day of school on Saturday. She was supposed to be here yesterday."

Izzy hated the whine creeping into her voice, but she couldn't help it. Nothing was happening the way it was supposed to.

"I'm sorry, Iz." He tried to put his arm around her.

Izzy shook it off. "What's going on, Dad? Why are these people here?" Izzy didn't know how to explain to her father that she wanted him home—all of him—and that Afghanistan was getting in the way. "Does Mom know about this? What did you do with her stuff?

She's not going to want to move home if there are strangers living upstairs."

Dad sighed. "Of course Mom knows."

"But why are they *here*? I mean, don't they want to be in their own country?"

"Of course they do, Iz. But when the Taliban learned that Hassan was helping the Americans, he wasn't safe. And neither was his family. They were able to get a Special Immigrant Visa to come to the US."

"If he's a doctor, why was he working as an interpreter?"

"The Taliban have done horrible things to their own people. Hassan and many other Afghan men worked with the United States to fight against them."

All of this talk of war was making Izzy's head hurt. "But I thought they moved to Connecticut."

"They did, but . . . it didn't work out." He looked around the yard. "And I really need the help."

Izzy followed her father's gaze, staring at the line of boats, high and dry on wooden blocks.

"He's a doctor *and* a boat mechanic?"

"No. But it would take a long time for him to get the certifications to be a doctor here. He doesn't have the time or money to do that. He needs a job now." Izzy's dad looked hard at her. "Why are you acting this way, Izzy? Hassan is my friend. He saved my life."

Izzy crossed her arms. "Mom's not going to like this."

"Well, Mom's not here and they *are*."

Izzy could hear the tone of her father's voice change as if that switch flipped again—the one where Dad went from normal to losing his temper.

She bit the inside of her cheek as she watched him close his eyes and turn away from her, quietly counting to himself as he took deep breaths.

Izzy's frustration deflated like a popped balloon. She hadn't meant to upset her dad.

He took one last long, deep breath, then smiled his half smile.

"Come on," he finally said. "Let's celebrate the first day of school. Starenka made a cake."

But Izzy didn't feel like celebrating. "I'll be there in a minute," she said.

Her dad tilted his head at her as if he was trying to look inside her brain. "Okay. But come soon."

Chapter 6

Izzy scowled as she watched her father rejoin the group. Dr. Haidary was lifting the pot of corn onto the burner. Dad stood near another pot that was boiling over into the grass. Starenka and Mrs. Haidary pinned a tablecloth to the picnic table and the boys set it with lobster crackers and napkins. Izzy's stomach rumbled as she stared at the steaming pots, but she didn't want to eat any of it. Somehow, joining them for dinner would be the same as saying *This is all okay!* when none of it was okay. Plus, she was worried she might say or do the wrong thing, which would set her dad off again.

Izzy felt her phone vibrate with a new text. She pulled it out of her back pocket.

Piper: Sup Sea Stars?

"Cosmic," Izzy said to Flotsam. "It's like she can sense something is wrong."

Izzy: can u meet at sea star HQ? Urgent
Piper: perfect timing. parents out. on my way
Zelda: kk

"Come on, Flotsam," Izzy said. She made sure her dad was busy before making her way to the skiff. But when she climbed inside, Flotsam barked.

"Shush, Flotsam," she said. "Get in!"

Flotsam barked again.

Izzy looked up, hoping everyone was too busy with their happy party to notice, but she was wrong. Her father had turned and was walking toward her.

Flotsam whined but wouldn't get in the boat.

"Fine, if you want to stay—then stay." Izzy untied the rope and pushed off. She lowered the engine into the water and yanked the cord until it rumbled to life. Murky silt churned as she backed out.

"Izzy!" her father called.

I'll pretend I didn't hear him, she thought as she brought the boat around the pier. That's when she saw a figure on the other side by the gas pump. It was the girl, Sitara. She was staring at Izzy with her intense brown eyes.

Izzy was confused. *Is she curious? Angry? Jealous?* She tried to look away, but Sitara's eyes were like magnets, holding her gaze.

As Izzy neared the fuel dock, Sitara held up her hand like a stop sign. "Take me with you," she said.

Izzy didn't know what came over her, but she navigated the boat against the dock.

Sitara stood there.

"Well?" Izzy said. "Get in if you're getting in."

Sitara squatted as if she was going to jump into the boat.

"Not like that!" Izzy reached for her. "Hold my hand and step into the center or you'll capsize us."

Sitara grabbed Izzy's arm a little too tightly. She stepped in and the boat rocked.

"Sit down! In the middle," Izzy said.

Sitara sat. Her scarf slid back, revealing long, silky black hair. She yanked it back in place, then smiled. "Go!" she shouted.

Izzy pointed the boat toward the channel as Dr. Haidary stepped onto the dock, sending it rocking back and forth. For a second, Izzy worried that he was going to fall in.

"No! Stop! Sitara cannot swim!" he yelled.

"You can't swim?" Izzy asked Sitara.

Dr. Haidary was halfway to the fuel dock, followed by Izzy's father and Flotsam. "Come back!" they were shouting.

Flotsam's barks pierced the air.

Izzy shook her head. *Why did I stop?* How could she meet the Sea Stars to discuss her problem if her problem was with her? She glared at Sitara as she directed the boat back to the fuel dock.

"Toss me the bowline, Izzy," Dad said. He grabbed it, holding the skiff tight against the pier. Dr. Haidary started to climb in after Sitara, but her father stopped him.

"Let me help, Hassan," her dad said.

Mrs. Haidary stood at the edge of the parking lot, wringing her hands.

Izzy's dad reached for Sitara. "Take my hand," he said calmly.

When Sitara was safely on the pier, Dr. Haidary ushered her toward her mother, scolding her in rapid Pashto the whole way.

Izzy's dad shook his head. "What's gotten into you, Izzy? Sitara could have gotten seriously hurt. You need to think."

"I didn't tell her to get into the boat." Izzy's eyes welled with tears, but she was too angry to cry. "Plus, the pond is shallow. If she fell out, she could stand up. What are they so mad about?"

"Afghanistan is a landlocked country. To them, the pond feels like an ocean. It doesn't feel safe."

Izzy opened her mouth, but nothing came out.

"Bring the skiff back to its slip."

"But I need to meet—"

Her father's hard stare silenced her. A blood vessel seemed to pulse in his temple. *They've been here less than a day and Dad's already lost his temper twice*, Izzy thought.

"What you need to do is return the boat and join us for dinner." He spun on his heel, heading toward the others, who were still fussing over Sitara. Izzy watched the pier rock back and forth under his angry footsteps.

She navigated the skiff to its slip, making the turns as wide as possible. *The longer it takes to get there*, she thought, *the better*. She gazed across the pond in the direction of the barrier beach, where she knew Piper and Zelda were waiting for her.

When the boat was secured, she pulled out her cell phone to text them, but her phone was dead.

The picnic table was set with platters of lobsters and steamers, salad, corn on the cob, and baked potatoes. Starenka had fixed a plate for her. "Sit, Isabella," she said.

"I need to charge my phone first," she said as she headed toward the shop.

Her dad held out his hand. "Not so fast. Hand it over."

Izzy looked up at him. "What?"

"For taking Sitara on the boat."

Izzy was so embarrassed that her dad was scolding her in front of everyone. She wanted to scream,

It wasn't me. It was her! But she could feel everyone's eyes on her. She handed the phone to her father, who tucked it into his shirt pocket.

"Let's eat," he said as if everything was fine.

But nothing was fine.

As everyone else dug in, Izzy stared at her lobster, feeling as if nothing would be fine ever again.

Later, in their kitchen, Izzy helped Starenka crack and pick meat out of the uneaten lobsters. Her dad was outside washing out the pots.

"The Haidarys didn't eat any lobster," Izzy said as she picked up a piece of meat to pop into her mouth.

Starenka gently swatted her hand. "That's tomorrow's lunch."

"Fine."

"Did I tell you the story when my mama came here from Czechoslovakia?" Starenka said as she cracked open a claw.

Izzy rolled her eyes. Her grandmother loved to tell her "olden days" stories that usually were about someone not having enough food, getting sick, working really hard, or all three. Izzy wasn't in the mood.

85

"My mother was very poor and had to stay on the bottom of the ship that brought her family to the United Sates. Steerage, they called it," Starenka began. "My grandmother was sick on that boat, so Mama had to take care of her baby brother—you remember, Uncle Viktor."

Izzy nodded.

"Well, the rich children on the top deck would throw coins down to steerage so they could watch the poor kids swarm to pick them up. But Mama was holding Viktor so she couldn't get any money. She started to cry."

"That's mean," Izzy said as she cracked open a tail.

"But one lady felt sorry for Mama. She called to her and tossed her a banana." Starenka pretended to toss something. "Mama had never seen a banana before, so she bit into it—right into the yellow skin." Starenka pretended to chomp hard with her fake teeth as if she were eating corn on the cob. "But right away she spit it out because it tasted bad. She thought the lady had tricked her." Starenka laughed.

Izzy shook her head, but she couldn't help but smile too. Starenka got very animated in her stories.

Starenka held up her finger as if to make a point. "It is like this with the Haidarys," she said. "The lobster is the same to them as the banana was to my mother."

Izzy hadn't thought about it that way. A lobster must look pretty strange to someone who'd never seen one before.

The door opened and Dad walked in. From under the table, Flotsam lifted his head and yawned. Then he rolled over and went back to sleep.

Izzy studied her father. He had dark circles under his eyes, and the side of his face that didn't smile frowned more than usual. She suddenly felt guilty for how she'd acted earlier.

"I'm really sorry, Dad," she said.

He took a seat at the table.

Izzy walked over. "Can I please have my phone back?"

He shook his head. "One week, Izzy."

"A week? But I can't—" She thought about Zelda and Piper. How long had they waited for her before they gave up and went home? Tears welled in her eyes. *How many times am I going to cry today?* she wondered.

Starenka handed Dad a plate of lobster. "Eat, Vincent; you hardly had any supper."

"I'm okay, Ma." He pushed the plate away.

Izzy gazed longingly at the phone peeking from her dad's shirt pocket. She needed to call the Sea Stars. She needed to explain. "Can I at least—" Izzy gulped. "I need to text Zelda. For school."

"I said no!" His voice began to take on that angry tone again. "You know what Hassan means to me, Izzy," Dad said. "You know he—"

"I know! He saved your life. Now he's brought his family here to ruin mine." She hated the words coming from her mouth, but she couldn't seem to stop them. Her father was acting as if she'd robbed a bank or something. She thought back to an old movie she'd once watched called *Invasion of the Body Snatchers*. In the movie, everyone looked the same on the outside, but aliens controlled their feelings on the inside. That's how Izzy felt right then. Part of her wanted to wrap her arms around her dad and say she was sorry. The other part didn't want to talk to him ever again.

She stormed out of the kitchen, shut her bedroom door, and flopped onto her bed. Flotsam scratched to come in. She got up and let him slip inside before shutting the door again. He jumped on the bed.

An image of Piper and Zelda sitting by the headquarters waiting for her flashed through her brain. She wished Dad had gotten a landline for the apartment or at least the shop, but he needed to save money, so he only had his cell phone.

She pulled the key from her pocket and turned it over in her palm, feeling its worn spots. Then she placed it gently on her nightstand. She changed into her pajamas and crawled under the covers. Flotsam settled across the foot of her bed.

"At least I have you," she said to him. Then she rolled over. Staring up at her sea star mobile, she worried what Zelda would say about her no-show. "After today, you might be the only friend I have left."

Chapter 7

The next morning, as Izzy spread Fluff on her bread, Dad came in and kissed her on top of the head. Then he gripped her shoulders, turning her until she faced him.

"Is there something you want to say to me?" he asked.

Izzy cleared her throat. "I'm sorry, Dad. I shouldn't have taken Sitara on the boat."

"You shouldn't have taken the boat in the first place."

Izzy turned back, dipping the knife into peanut

butter. "And you should have warned me they were coming."

Her dad walked over to the counter and lifted the coffeepot. "Don't be sassy, Izzy. I thought it would be a good surprise, but you have made it abundantly clear you would have preferred some notice." He replaced the pot on the burner. It sizzled.

She felt him watching her.

"You need to wear a life jacket from now on when you're on the pond," he said as he sipped his coffee.

"What? I'm a great swimmer! Plus, the pond barely comes above my waist."

"Except the channel and the breachway."

"I'm barely in the channel and I don't go near the breachway."

"We need to set a good example." Dad's cell phone rang. He looked at it. "It's Skip. I need to take this." Her father stepped into the next room.

"There must be a hundred texts from the Sea Stars," Izzy said, shaking the knife at Flotsam. He licked his lips. She finished spreading peanut butter and wrapped her sandwich.

"This is the second time in a week . . . " Izzy heard

her father's voice rise in its post-Afghanistan angry tone.

She grabbed the Honey Nut Cheerios and poured some into a bowl. She liked her cereal better with no milk.

"Well, I understand," her dad continued. "But explain that to the owners. The bite's on and they want their boats in the water. I understand you've got a lot going on, but . . . Yes, okay. I'll see you at nine."

Her father's mouth was a tight line when he returned.

Izzy took a bite. "Where's Skip?"

"Missing in action." He looked out the window. "Thank goodness for Hassan. He's still learning, but he's been working on the Whaler's engine since the sun came up. I think we'll have it figured out today."

Izzy finished her cereal, washed the bowl, and put it in the rack. "Um, Dad. They're having a thing where the school clubs and sports teams talk about what they do to get people to join. I need to go to make sure Piper and Zelda and I get in the same club." She paused. "So I need my phone."

"Sorry, Iz. At least one more day."

Last night he'd said a week. He was already softening. Izzy gave him a big frown anyway.

"I think Mrs. McLaughlin, your old art teacher, is doing drawing club," he said.

"Really?" That would at least make up for missing art class.

"What time do you want me to pick you up?" he asked.

"I don't know," she said. "That's why I need my phone, so I can text you when I find out."

"I'll call the school and ask."

"Dad, please, I'll only use it to—"

Before Izzy could finish her sentence, there was a knock on the door. Dad opened it. "Perfect timing, Sitara. Izzy's leaving now."

Izzy's mouth fell open. Her dad gave her a laser stare and she shut it.

He looked at his watch. "Well, you two better get going. The bus will be at the end of the road any second."

Izzy grabbed her bag, then turned to glare at her father. "I wouldn't know that," she said. "Since I don't have my phone."

"Thank you for showing me where we'll get picked up for school," Sitara said as they made their way to the bus stop. She was wearing jeans, a black long-sleeved shirt, and a silky blue headscarf. The temperature was supposed to reach ninety by noon.

"I'm going anyway." Izzy stared at the scarf wrapped snugly around Sitara's face. "Are you going to wear that to school?"

"My hijab? Of course."

"You're going to be hot."

"I'll be fine."

Izzy shook her head ever so slightly.

As they approached the bus stop, the few kids waiting stared at Sitara. Two girls started to whisper. Part of Izzy wanted to say, *I told you to take it off.*

The bus approached, chuffing to a stop. Its lights flashed red. Sitara grabbed Izzy's arm. Izzy glanced at her, wanting to yank it back, but at the same time seeing something in Sitara's large brown eyes that told her to let her be.

As they made their way onto the bus, Izzy said, "You're going to have to let go of my arm or we won't fit."

"Sorry," Sitara said as she released her grip.

They slid into an empty seat. As the bus made its way around the neighborhood, Sitara stared straight ahead. When they stopped at the corner of Rosewood and Moonstone, the scent of honeysuckle tickled Izzy's nose, reminding her to look for the little blue cottage. Her stomach dropped when she saw it.

In the corner of the lot next to the SOLD sign sat a giant yellow excavator.

The bus doors folded shut and the bus chugged onward.

"Told ya," Roger said as he fell into the seat behind her.

Apollo was next to him. "By the end of the month you won't even know that house ever existed."

Izzy wrinkled her nose at Apollo's words and the fact that his breath smelled as though he'd had Doritos for breakfast.

But Apollo was too busy studying Sitara to notice. "Who are you?" he asked.

"My name is Sitara. I'm new."

"We can see that." Apollo snorted.

"What are you wearing on your head?" Roger asked.

Sitara put a hand to her scarf. "It's my hijab. I wear it because I'm Muslim."

"What'd you say? You wear it because you're a terrorist?" Apollo shouted in mock terror. Then he fell back, laughing.

Izzy wished she could melt into her seat.

Roger punched him in the arm. "Shut up, Apollo," he said.

Izzy felt her ears get hot. She turned to Sitara. "Do you *have* to keep that on?" she asked in a low voice. "I mean, are your parents making you wear it?"

"My father told me it was my choice to wear hijab to school. He was worried students would bother me because they don't understand." Sitara coolly stared forward. "But I want to wear hijab. It is part of my religion."

Izzy stared at Sitara's profile. Part of her was impressed that she didn't seem to care what anyone thought, but she was worried too. What would Zelda and Piper make of her?

Fifteen minutes later, they pulled into the middle school. The girls stepped off the bus. Heads turned as Sitara walked through the crowd. Izzy searched for Zelda and Piper, but she couldn't find them anywhere.

"My mother told me I should introduce myself to the principal," Sitara said. "Can you bring me there?"

Izzy gave one last scan of the kids pushing their way inside. No Zelda. No Piper. She nodded at Sitara. "Yeah. It's right here."

Inside the main office, the principal, Mrs. Cook, was making photocopies. "Good morning, ladies."

"My name is Sitara Haidary. I'm new to this school."

"Ah," Mrs. Cook said. "Welcome!" She turned to Izzy. "You must be Isabella Mancini?"

Izzy nodded.

"Your dad called to say that you'd be happy to show Sitara around today."

"Well," Izzy said. "We're probably in different classes."

Mrs. Cook placed a piece of paper on the counter. "This is Sitara's schedule."

Izzy studied it. They were in the same classes except language arts.

"Okay."

"Great, let us know if you need anything." Mrs. Cook returned to her copies.

As they made their way down the hall, Izzy paused to check for Zelda and Piper at their lockers, but they weren't there. Along the way, there was more pointing and staring. Izzy couldn't tell if Sitara noticed. If she did, she didn't let on.

"What number is your locker?" Izzy asked.

"Eight seventy-five," Sitara said.

"I'm eight seventy-six. You're next to me." They reached the lockers. "Do you want me to show you how to—"

But with a few turns, Sitara had her locker open.

Izzy tried hers.

Nothing.

Sitara put her lunch away. "Would you like some help?"

"I got it," Izzy said, pressing extra hard at each number.

The first bell rang. The locker still wouldn't open.

"Fine, you try," Izzy said, frustrated. "The combination is three-twenty-fourteen."

Sitara spun the dial. The locker opened.

"How'd you do that?"

Sitara shrugged.

Izzy put her lunch away. "Okay, well, tech ed is right here." She shut the door with a clang.

Zelda and Piper were sitting in front of the computer when they walked in.

Piper leapt up and gathered Izzy in a tight hug. "Are you okay? Why haven't you answered any of my texts?"

"You guys, I'm so sorry!" Izzy gushed. "I got in trouble and my dad wouldn't let me take the skiff and then he took my phone away and—"

Izzy realized Zelda wasn't listening. She was staring at Sitara, who had pushed her way into their circle.

"Um, hello?" Zelda's eyebrow arched.

"I'm sorry," Izzy said. "This is Sitara . . . and these are my best friends, Zelda and Piper."

Piper gave a small wave.

Zelda leaned close to Izzy and whispered, "Does she speak English?"

Izzy cringed, knowing Sitara must have heard.

"Sitara and her family are living on the third-floor

apartment at the marina . . . well, I guess until they find their own place."

Sitara opened her mouth as if to say something when Mr. Cantor joined them. "Miss Haidary, welcome to tech ed," he said with perfect pronunciation. "I'm sure Miss Mancini will explain how everything works."

Izzy glanced at the assignment board. Next to SCRIPT she saw MANCINI/HAIDARY. Piper and Zelda were assigned to anchor again. She breathed a sigh of relief.

Roger walked in. "Yes!" he said, pumping his fist in the air. "I get to do camera again!"

"I like to have everyone get comfortable at a job before I change them," Mr. Cantor said. "But don't get too comfortable."

Zelda tugged on Piper's sleeve. "Come on," she said. "Let's get ready."

Izzy watched them join Taylor in the control room. The three girls huddled over the equipment.

"What do we do now?" Sitara asked.

"Um." Izzy bit her lip. "We . . . um . . . we need to write what Zelda and Piper are going to say."

They took their seats in front of the computer. Izzy

lifted a paper from the bin labeled ANNOUNCEMENTS. "This is where teachers put things they want us to include in the news. This one is about the activities fair after school today."

She couldn't help but peek into the control room to see what Zelda and Piper were doing. Taylor was applying lip gloss to Zelda. It wasn't working and the three were laughing.

"There's an astronomy club," Sitara said, reading the paper.

Izzy stared at the computer screen. Maybe if no one could write the script as well as she did, she could keep that job permanently and never have to anchor. Suddenly she felt pressure to come up with a perfect sea star question. *I know*, she thought, and began to type.

Piper and Zelda emerged from the control room wearing sparkly eye makeup like Taylor. Now they looked like high school students too.

"Are you done, Izzy?" Zelda said.

Izzy nodded as she clicked SUBMIT.

"Get in your places, everyone!" Mr. Cantor yelled.

He held his hand high. "Five, four." He lowered his

fingers . . . *three, two, one*, then pointed at Roger. The light on the camera blinked green.

Zelda flashed a glossy pink smile. "Good morning. It's Wednesday, September fifth, and this is your Shoreline Regional Middle School news," she said. "Today is National Cheese Pizza Day."

"For lunch there will be BLT burgers and, of course, cheese pizza," Piper said.

"On this day in history, in 1977, NASA launched the *Voyager 1* probe from Florida. It is currently the farthest man-made object in space," Zelda said.

"The Shoreline Regional Middle School Activities Fair is after school in the gym. Stop by to learn about the many clubs and activities our school has to offer," Piper said.

"The answer to yesterday's question is . . . echinoderms," Zelda said. "Sea stars are not fish, they're echinoderms."

"Finally," Piper said, "we will leave you with a new trivia question. Sea stars are able to adapt to almost any kind of ocean environment and can be found all over the world. Mostly they live close to the ocean's surface, which is why they sometimes wash up on-shore."

"Sea stars have a variety of ways to protect themselves from predators," Zelda said.

"What is one way sea stars protect themselves from their enemies?" Piper asked.

"Answer, next time."

"Smooth Operator" began to play.

"This is Piper Grenier." She turned, grinning at Zelda.

"And Zelda Akins."

"Signing off," they sang together. "See you tomorrow for more Shoreline Regional Middle School news."

Mr. Cantor pointed to Roger and the camera went dark. "That's a wrap," he said.

Zelda and Piper removed their mics and bounded out of their seats.

Izzy stood up. "You guys were great," she said. But they didn't seem to hear her as they made their way to the control room.

Chapter 8

By the time Izzy took her seat in science that after-noon, she felt hot and tired. She'd had about enough of Sitara being glued to her side all day—especially when she had to miss lunch with Piper and Zelda so she could bring her to guidance.

When Sitara sat in the seat Izzy had been saving for Zelda, she thought she was going to lose it.

Zelda gave Izzy her best *Seriously?* eyebrow arch be-fore moving to the back.

Since science had dropped yesterday, this was their first time meeting Ms. Sardo, who stood at the front of the room thumbing through a stack of papers. She didn't look like any science teacher Izzy had ever seen before. She wore spiky black heels, capri pants, and a T-shirt that said SCIENCE CHICK with an image of a baby chick wearing the same thick glasses that she wore. Her long brown hair was pulled into a sleek ponytail.

When the bell rang, she put the papers down. "Welcome, sixth graders!" she said. "We have an exciting year ahead of us, and we're going to begin at the bottom of the sea."

She pointed a remote at the board. An image that looked like a map of the earth materialized, but instead of continents, it showed a big green bloblike shape plopped in the middle of blue water.

"Does anyone know what this green shape is?"

Izzy sat up. "Pangaea," she whispered under her breath.

"Anyone?" Ms. Sardo inquired.

Izzy did not raise her hand.

Ms. Sardo smiled at the blob as if it was the most beautiful thing she'd ever seen. "This," she said, directing a laser pointer at it, "is what our world looked like two hundred million years ago when the land-masses still formed a supercontinent called Pangaea." She directed the pointer at the blue all around it. "Pangaea was surrounded by a global ocean called Panthalassa. The landmass kept breaking apart until it formed the continents we know today, as well as the Atlantic and Indian Oceans."

"Where are we on there?" Roger asked.

Ms. Sardo clicked the remote and the blob began to break apart—pieces shifted and moved until it took the shape of the continents on a modern-day map. Ms. Sardo shined the pointer along the southern coast of New England. "Here we are," she said.

"Cool!" kids exclaimed.

"In 1912, the theory of Pangaea was proposed by a meteorologist named Alfred Wegener. The idea started when Wegener asked a simple question: Why?"

Ms. Sardo clicked, and the screen showed an image of a thin man with slicked-back hair and a slight mus-tache. "While studying an atlas of the world, Wegener noticed how the continents seemed as if they could fit together like pieces in a puzzle."

As she spoke, Ms. Sardo picked up the stack of

paper she'd been flipping through earlier and walked around handing one to each student. When Izzy got hers, she saw it showed outlines of the continents.

"At the time," Ms. Sardo continued, "most American scientists believed that the continents were fixed—that they didn't move at all. However, Wegener theorized that the continents had once been joined, but had drifted apart horizontally. He called his theory continental drift. For thirty years he developed his theory, writing several books on the subject. But scientists repeatedly dismissed his ideas because he was challenging what they'd accepted as fact."

Ms. Sardo stood in the front of the room again. "Today, we are going to travel back in time. I want you to cut out the continents, and then I want you to see what Wegener saw by fitting them together into the supercontinent Pangaea."

As Izzy started cutting, Sitara leaned over and whispered, "You knew the answer. Why didn't you raise your hand?"

Izzy shrugged. "I wasn't sure I was right."

When she finished cutting, Izzy rearranged the pieces. It was cool how Africa tucked almost perfectly in between North and South America and how Antarctica, India, and Australia fit snugly below Africa.

Ms. Sardo moved around the room. "You got it," she said to Izzy as she passed her desk.

When everyone was finished, Ms. Sardo asked, "So, was Wegener right? Do you agree with his theory?" Kids raised their hands. "John Z? What do you think?"

"Yeah, I mean, it looks like it, the way the continents fit so easily together."

"Very good. For the most part Wegener was right. The continents do move," Ms. Sardo said. "And I find it interesting that he was looking at the same continents that all those other scientists were looking at, yet only he was willing to look past what everyone believed to find the real truth."

"So continental drift is real? Are we still moving?" Chelsea asked.

"No and yes," Ms. Sardo said. "Wegener was correct that the continents moved, but he was wrong about the way they did it. What really happens is that the plates on the earth's crust float on the mantle." She clicked the remote and the words PLATE TECTONICS appeared. "Wegener's theories led to the study of plate tectonics, which is now considered a fundamental principle of earth science. But"—she paused—"it took the work of an oceanographic cartographer to prove that." She winked. "But that's for next week."

Izzy sat up. She was pretty sure Ms. Sardo was talking about Marie Tharp, the woman who was the subject of the book *Soundings* that she had found at the marina and who had inspired her to map the pond.

"We are going to spend the rest of class watching a film on Wegener and his theory of Pangaea and continental drift. Make sure to take good notes. There will be a handout for homework."

After the video, Ms. Sardo held up more papers. "Grab a homework sheet on your way out. It's due tomorrow."

Izzy was putting her notebook away when Zelda sidled up to her desk. "Piper's not going to the activities fair," she said.

"What? How are we supposed to get into the same club if one of us isn't there?"

Sitara moved next to Izzy.

Zelda scanned her up and down. "I have to go to my locker," she said. "I'll see you later."

Before Izzy could say anything else, Sitara said, "Where do we go now?"

"Oh, Sitara," Izzy said. "You need to make the bus!"

"No, it's okay. I can go to the activities fair with you."

"But you can't stay after school without permission."

"My guidance counselor phoned my father. He said I could stay."

"Oh." Izzy sighed, wondering when she'd get a chance to be alone with the Sea Stars.

In the hallway, Izzy found Piper at her locker.

"Why aren't you going to the activities fair?" she asked.

Piper bit her lip. "My mom says I have to go straight home after school." She grabbed her backpack.

"Tutor?"

Piper shook her head. "I gotta go." She ran off before Izzy could say goodbye.

Inside the gym, rows of tables were decorated with balloons and posters explaining each club. Izzy scanned the noisy room.

"What are you looking for?" Sitara asked.

"I thought Zelda was going to meet me here." She shrugged. "I guess we should walk around."

At the drawing club table, Izzy saw Mrs. McLaughlin.

"Hi, Izzy," she said. "Nice to see you. Will you be joining us?"

"Yeah, definitely," she said. "But I'm waiting for my friend Zelda so we can sign up together."

"Well, don't wait too long. It's filling up." Mrs. McLaughlin looked at Sitara. "How about you?"

"I think I'd like to do astronomy club," Sitara said.

"Sounds fun. You guys should check that out. I'll see you soon, Izzy."

As they moved from table to table, Izzy kept her eyes peeled for Zelda. While Sitara was busy signing up at the astronomy table, Izzy found Zelda at cross-country talking to Taylor. She raced over there.

"Hey," Izzy said. "I've been looking for you."

"I signed up for cross-country," Zelda said. "Taylor is the captain."

"Oh," Izzy said. "I thought we were doing drawing club."

Zelda glanced at Taylor. "That's so fifth grade, Izzy."

Taylor was busy going over the meet schedule with some kids. Izzy watched Zelda watch her.

"You used to like art," Izzy said.

Zelda pretended to examine her nails. "In kindergarten, maybe."

"Oh," Izzy said. She glanced at the drawing club table, hoping there was still room. "So, why couldn't Piper stay?"

Zelda didn't look up from her nails. "Didn't she tell you?"

"No."

"She had to go home because of you."

"Me?" Izzy's voice squeaked.

"Last night, when you didn't come right away, I wanted to leave. But Piper said, 'Izzy wouldn't have texted if she didn't need us.' So we ended up waiting for like an hour."

"I did need you. But what's that got to do with the activities fair?"

"You know what Mrs. Grenier's like. Piper got grounded because she wasn't home when her mom and dad got back from dinner."

"I—I didn't know." Izzy swallowed hard. "But it wasn't my fault."

"You should have made sure you could go before you texted," Zelda snapped.

Izzy opened her mouth to say something, but was so confused by the way Zelda was acting that she changed her mind. Taylor had finished talking with the students and had started to pack up the table.

"I can help," Zelda said. She began gathering flyers.

Izzy awkwardly watched for a moment, then she walked back to find Mrs. McLaughlin.

"I want to sign up now."

"Izzy, I was looking for you!" Mrs. McLaughlin said. "I'm sorry, we're filled, but you can join the wait list."

"Oh," Izzy said as her heart sank.

Later, as Sitara and Izzy waited in front of the school for her dad, Zelda was in deep conversation with Taylor.

Izzy heard her telling Taylor what an "amazing" team captain she must be, and asking for advice on how to run faster. Izzy had never seen Zelda run. Ever. When Izzy's dad rolled up in the marina pickup, she didn't try to say goodbye.

"Where's Flotsam?" she asked as she climbed into the cab. She scooched close to her father to make room for Sitara, who was having a hard time climbing in. Dad reached over Izzy to help her.

"It's a big step," he said, hoisting her up.

Sitara plopped next to Izzy. Her hijab fell askew, revealing a few strands of hair that she quickly tucked away.

"Where's Flotsam?" Izzy asked again.

"It'd be a little crowded with him, don't you think?"

"He could have ridden in back." Izzy frowned.

"Not on Route One," her dad said.

The air-conditioning in the truck didn't work, so the windows were open. Sitara seemed to enjoy the breeze as they made their way onto the highway.

"How was school?" Dad shouted.

Izzy held her hand up to her ear. "I can't hear you." Really, the day had left her feeling like her skin didn't fit right. She wanted to get home and peel it off like a bad outfit. Right then, a boat ride on the pond seemed like a perfect idea.

Chipped stones crunched under the truck's tires as they drove into the marina's boatyard. Flotsam barked and came galloping toward them. Izzy could tell he was disappointed that he didn't get to go. He jumped on the door as Sitara tried to open it.

Izzy's dad got out and walked around. "Down, Flotsam," he said. "Sorry, Sitara." He held Flotsam's collar. "You can open your door now."

Sitara slid out. Izzy followed.

"Your father's in the mechanic's workshop and your mother's upstairs," Izzy's dad told Sitara. "She's been cooking up a storm all day."

"Thank you for the ride," Sitara said.

As Izzy followed her inside and up the stairs, a spicy scent filled her nose. It didn't smell bad—just different. Izzy wasn't in the mood for different.

When the girls got to the second floor, Izzy said, "See you later," before ducking into her apartment.

After a moment, she could hear the door open on the third floor and Mrs. Haidary greet Sitara in Pashto. Even though Izzy didn't know the words, she understood what they were saying. *Hi, sweetheart, how was your day? I missed you!* She definitely understood the happiness she heard in Mrs. Haidary's voice.

Izzy stared at her own empty kitchen, wondering

what was so important at Loretta's Kitchen that her mom couldn't leave. She dragged her bag toward her room as if it held the weight of the day.

Inside her bedroom, Izzy closed the door, then leaned back against it. She had decorated her new room to look almost the same as her old bedroom. Now she flopped onto her bed and stared up at her sea star mobile as it danced in the breeze from the opened window. Dad had painted the walls a powdery sky blue, and her *Endless Summer* poster hung over her bed.

She turned to look at the World Ocean Floor Panorama she'd taped to her wall. It was a copy of an actual map that Marie Tharp developed with the sounding data collected by her partner, Bruce Heezen, and other scientists. Before Marie Tharp, scientists believed the ocean floor was flat and smooth. Her map proved that it was made of mountains and valleys and ridges—even volcanoes.

Izzy got up and walked closer to examine Marie's map. No matter how many times she looked at it, the intricate details gave her goose bumps. She traced her finger along the Mid-Atlantic Ridge, which ran like a backbone around the world.

Next to it, Izzy had posted the outline of her own growing map of the pond floor. Marie had used data from sonar measurements. Since Izzy couldn't do that, she researched what scientists had used before sonar and discovered they'd used sounding lines marked with scraps of leather or calico that had been tied every second or third fathom. Like Izzy's knotted string, the original sounding lines were weighted with lead so they'd sink to the bottom of the ocean.

Izzy had mapped most of the pond by herself, bringing Zelda and Piper with her only once. Zelda had complained through most of it.

"Are you almost done?" Zelda had said over and over, refusing to set foot in the murky water. "Let's go surfing."

Piper started getting seasick.

After only fifteen minutes on the pond, Izzy brought them to Brogee's. "You guys go," she said. "I want to finish around Horseshoe Point today."

"Why do you like this so much?" Zelda had asked.

Izzy had shrugged. "I don't know. I just think it's really cool. When I look below the surface, I see stuff that no one else knows is there. I feel like I'm doing something important."

Izzy moved back to her bed and closed her eyes as the sounds of the marina drifted over her—the rush of boats coming and going, voices in the harbor calling out, the occasional caw of a seagull, and the splash of water as owners hosed down their boats.

She knew her dad wouldn't let her take the skiff out until her homework was finished. She sat up. *All I have is the science worksheet*, she thought. *If I get it done quickly, maybe he'll let me go.*

But after taking everything out of her bag and flipping through her notebook, she couldn't find the handout.

The front door of their apartment slammed. "Izzy!" her father called. She heard Flotsam lapping water from his bowl and the sound of her dad's work boots clomping toward her bedroom. A knock and her door opened. "How did Sitara do today?" he asked.

Izzy let her head flop back down on the bed. "I don't know. Fine."

"Do you have homework?"

"Science. Can I have my phone back? I need to call Zelda. I have an important homework question." She also had an important *Are you really mad at me or were you just acting weird?* question. Asking Zelda to text her a photo of the homework gave her a good excuse to call.

Her father stared at the ceiling. Izzy could tell he was struggling.

"Please, Dad. I really need it for school."

"Okay," he finally said. "I guess I made my point." He pulled the phone from his pocket. "But, from now on, you need to ask before you take off on the skiff," he said. "It's not only us here now. You made Hassan and Meena very nervous. Also, you have to wear a life jacket like you're supposed to."

Izzy stared hard at her father. She was starting to feel as if he cared more about the Haidarys than her. "I'm a good swimmer."

Her father shook his head. "It's the law, Iz. I should have made you do it sooner." He held the phone in front of her like a bribe. "Promise?"

"Fine."

He tossed the phone and Izzy caught it. She scrambled to plug it into its charger, then sat back on the bed. "Okay, well, I'm asking now," she said. "Can Flotsam and I go on the boat? I need to finish around the oyster farm and do Mack's Cove."

"Not today," her father said.

"Why not?"

"The Haidarys have invited us for dinner. Six o'clock." He grinned as if this were good news.

Izzy wrinkled her nose at the sharp smells coming from upstairs. "What if there's nothing for me to eat?"

Dad winked. "I guess you'll starve."

"Is Starenka coming?"

"No." He laughed. "She's at the Ocean Mist with her friends. They have money riding on the Sox-Braves game."

After Dad left, Flotsam jumped onto Izzy's bed and lay down. He nudged her with his nose to pet him.

"At least you still love me," she said.

Flotsam's fur was wet and he smelled fishy, but Izzy didn't care. She scratched behind his ears. After the phone had charged for a while, she rolled over to check it. A bunch of texts from the night before popped up.

Piper: Here

Zelda: Pipe and I are @ HQ. Where r u?

Piper: IIIIIZZZZZZZZZZYYYYYY?!?!?!?!?!

Zelda: leaving in 5 if u r not here

Piper: r u ok

Zelda: GTG

Piper: what happened?!?!?!?!

And then that morning:

Zelda: what up with last night

Piper: ur scaring me plz FT me

Izzy turned the phone off. She considered calling Piper, then remembered what Zelda had said about her getting grounded because of Izzy. *If Piper acts as mad at me as Zelda did, I'm going to lose it.*

Zelda had said doing the middle school news together would be the answer to everything. Izzy was starting to think it wasn't even the beginning.

Second Grade

In second grade, we had my birthday party on Brogee's Beach. Zelda and Piper came dressed as their favorite mermaids, which meant they were both Ariel.

But I was Oceania, a mermaid I'd created on my own.

Mom made mermaid tails for each of us from long pieces of felt. She made Oceania's extra sparkly with pretend diamonds and glitter seashells.

We spent the afternoon bodysurfing—waiting for a big wave and then diving in to ride it into shore. Forward and back. The waves sent me forward and the tide pulled me back. Ebb and flow. I was the wave and it was me. I couldn't tell where the ocean stopped and I began.

Mom always said that the ocean is full of energy. Right then, its energy coursed through my veins like a shooting star.

The day only got better, with ice pops, and Del's lem-onade, and pink birthday cake with pink frosting.

Zelda always gave the best birthday presents—that year it was a light pink camera that printed instant photos. Polaroid, Mom called it. She said it was retro. I thought it was the coolest thing ever. We took pictures of each other doing cartwheels in the water.

Later, Zelda wanted to wear my extra-sparkly mer-maid tail. When we switched, she became Oceania, and I was just a regular mermaid.

We all tried to squeeze into the Sea Star HQ, but that was the first time we didn't all fit. Mom says it was because we were grown up seven-year-olds now.

At first we took turns, but it was really only Piper and me taking turns. Zelda said Oceania couldn't leave her castle. But that was okay, because even then we were magical.

We were the Sea Stars, after all. We were going to be best friends forever.

Chapter 9

At six o'clock, Izzy followed her father upstairs, their arms loaded with gifts. Izzy's dad knocked on the Haidarys' door. Outside, five pairs of shoes in all different sizes were lined up in a row. Izzy's father had gone over the "rules" beforehand. Now Izzy followed his lead in taking off her flip-flops and leaving them outside.

Dr. Haidary opened the door. "Salâm! Welcome!" he said, smiling. "Please come in."

The apartment was thick with the smell of spices.

Sitara and her mother were busy chatting and stirring pots that bubbled softly on the stove.

Izzy handed Mrs. Haidary a bunch of black-eyed Susans that her father had collected.

"Manana!" Mrs. Haidary said, smiling as she accepted the bouquet. She wore a long yellow dress and hijab. Izzy smiled back, thinking she looked as summery as the flowers.

"I brought these fishing poles for Sitara, Hikmat, and Ali," her dad said. "Izzy's caught porgies and skipjacks off the dock here. Sometimes you can even get a decent striped bass."

"You are too generous, Vince," Dr. Haidary said. "They will love them. Now, please, everything has been prepared."

Izzy and her dad followed Dr. Haidary into their living room, which had been turned into a sit-on-the-floor dining room. A large brown leather square had been spread over the red carpet like a picnic blanket. Izzy counted at least ten platters of food spread across it. There seemed to be enough to feed all of Seabury. "Are more people coming?" she asked.

Dr. Haidary laughed. "No, no. This is what we call melmastiyâ. A gathering of our special guests. My wife is a talented cook. She has prepared our favorite dishes as a sign of respect and to thank you for your kindness. It is sort of like an Afghan buffet. You choose what you would like to eat."

"You've done too much," Izzy's father said.

Dr. Haidary smiled. "Please have a seat around the dëstârkhan." He pointed at the brown leather square. Red cushions were set around the room like a couch but on the ground.

"Salâm," Hikmat said as he entered the room.

Ali followed him. The boys stood shyly next to their father.

"Salâm," Izzy's father replied.

The boys sat politely across from Izzy and her father.

Soon Sitara came in carrying a steaming pot. Finally, Mrs. Haidary joined them.

"This is shorwâ," Sitara said as she scooped from the pot. She handed Izzy a bowl of an orange-colored soup. Izzy held it in front of her, not sure what to do. She glanced at her father, who had taken a piece of

126

the round, flat bread. He mixed it in the soup, then took a bite.

"This is excellent," he said.

Izzy wasn't so sure she'd like it. She put her bowl down, scanning the other dishes to see if anything looked familiar.

Sitara seemed to sense her uneasiness. She pointed to a dish. "This is qabuli palaw. It's one of our most popular dishes. It's made with rice and lamb and carrots. Oh, and what do you call those small dried fruit?"

"Raisins?"

"Yes, raisins!" Sitara said. "Would you like some?"

Izzy gave a small nod.

Sitara put some qabuli palaw on Izzy's plate.

Izzy's father nodded at her. She took a tiny bite. She was surprised the rice tasted sweet. "I like it!" She looked at her dad. "It's actually really good." She took a bigger bite.

Her dad laughed. "I agree."

"This is mantu," Sitara said.

The mantu looked like tiny dumplings covered in a white sauce and green leaves. She tried some, realizing the sauce was yogurt and the green leaves were mint. "I like this too," she said.

"And korma. Here, take some dodëy; it's our bread," Sitara said, reaching over Ali to grab a piece of the round bread. "And dip it into the korma." Sitara ate the food she had scooped up with the flat bread.

Izzy cautiously copied Sitara, dipping the bread into the korma and taking a bite. Her eyes got big. "Spicy!" she exclaimed, gulping the Sprite that Sitara had placed in front of her.

"I think you prefer the qabuli palaw," Sitara said.

Izzy grinned. "Can I try more of that?"

"Of course." Sitara piled more on her plate.

When Izzy couldn't eat one more bite, Mrs. Haidary brought out chai and baklava. As Sitara handed Izzy a cup, she leaned close and whispered, "Stay after; I want to show you a secret."

Izzy looked into Sitara's large brown eyes to see if she was serious. "Okay," she finally said.

After several pieces of sweet, nutty baklava, Izzy's father stood and began clearing plates.

Mrs. Haidary took them from him.

"No, please, you are our guest," Dr. Haidary kept repeating.

Finally, Izzy's dad gave up. "Thank you so much, Meena. Everything was delicious." He shook Dr. Haidary's hand, then turned to Izzy. "Ready to weigh anchor, Iz?"

Izzy glanced at Sitara, who continued to stare at her intently. "I'll be down soon," she said. "I need to talk to Sitara about our science homework."

Dad grinned. "Okay, see you downstairs."

Mrs. Haidary shooed the boys into their room. "Râsha," Izzy heard her say. The boys protested, but followed their mother.

Sitara grabbed Izzy's arm and pulled her into her bedroom, which was directly over Izzy's. Inside, she closed the door behind them, grinning ear to ear.

Sitara's bedroom was the same as Izzy's—but not the same.

Her "bed" was a cushion on the ground. There were no posters or colorful maps like Izzy had on her walls. The room's white paint had yellowed and was peeling in the corners. Clothes peeked out from a cardboard set of drawers. The only bit of color was a large blue book etched in gold that rested on a special stand next to Sitara's mattress.

"What is this?" Izzy asked, touching the book's cover. "It's so pretty."

"It's my Qur'ân. It's our Islamic sacred book." Sitara opened it from the back, showing Izzy the flowing writing.

"You can read that?"

"Of course," Sitara said. "It's written in Arabic."

"Wow," said Izzy, looking at the swirls and curls and dots of the writing. "It's beautiful."

"You read like this." Sitara pointed to the top right corner of the last page and traced her finger backward.

Izzy shook her head. It seemed impossible.

Sitara gently put the Qur'ân back.

"What's this next to it?" Izzy asked.

Sitara picked up a brown leather-bound book and opened it up to the last page. The writing looked like: زما نوم ستاره حیدري دی

"It's my special journal," she said. "It's where I keep my most personal thoughts."

Izzy looked at the writing. "That is so cool," she said. "I wish I could write like that."

"I can teach you," Sitara said. Then she turned and ducked inside her large walk-in closet.

Izzy put the journal back as Sitara began to pull things from her closet—a suitcase, an old vacuum cleaner, boxes.

"Um, I was actually serious about the homework," Izzy called to her. "I forgot my science handout at school. Can I take a picture of yours?"

When Sitara didn't answer, Izzy said, "Um, if you have to clean your closet now, maybe I should go. But if I can see the science sheet first . . ."

Sitara popped out of the closet. "Follow me," she said before disappearing back inside again.

Izzy sighed. She didn't have time for games, but she didn't want to get a zero on her first assignment in middle school.

When Sitara still didn't come out, Izzy peeked in after her. The closet was dark. "Sitara?" she called.

A head popped down from above. "Come on!" Sitara giggled.

"How did you get up there?" Izzy inched in deeper. As her eyes adjusted to the darkness, she saw there was a ladder secured to the back wall.

"Sitara?"

But Sitara was busy climbing the ladder.

Izzy put her hands on the rails and followed.

Above her, Sitara seemed to push on the ceiling. Cool air rushed in as she disappeared through a trapdoor.

When Izzy finally reached the top, she found herself looking across the marina's flat roof. Most of the spindle railings that had once encircled it had rotted and had fallen off.

Sitara was walking toward the chimney in the center. "Come on!" she called over her shoulder.

Izzy climbed out behind her but remained on her hands and knees.

"Over here!" Sitara giggled. She leaned against the chimney as if she were reclining on a beach chair.

Izzy crawled toward Sitara. The scratchy tar shingles scraped her knees and the palms of her hands. She was worried the roof wasn't strong enough to hold them and that they were about to plummet into the Haidarys' apartment below.

"It's okay," Sitara said.

Izzy stood, shakily drag-sliding her feet toward Sitara. She was careful to avoid a rusty satellite dish and a very-much-in-use weather antenna.

Her heart was pounding when she finally reached the chimney. Sitara extended her hand and Izzy gripped it, lowering herself down. She glanced back at the trapdoor they had emerged from. It had felt as if she had traveled miles to get there, but it was only a few feet away.

Izzy took a deep breath. The roof had captured the day's heat, and it felt warm against the cool night air.

"Isn't it perfect?" Sitara said. "I found the ladder last night when I was putting our things away."

Izzy looked around. "I've never seen the marina like this." The pond spread in front of them like a sheet of black glass. Crossword-puzzle-shaped piers reached into it as boats bobbed in their slips. She pointed at the horizon. "See those blinking red lights?" she said. "Those are windmills that make up the Block Island Wind Farm . . . and that flashing white light is from the North Lighthouse. Every lighthouse has a different flash so that boats can tell where they are by the flash. Technically, the North Light flashes for nine-tenths of a second followed by four point one seconds of dark, but you can count it like this—blink . . . one . . . two . . . three . . . four . . . blink," she said slowly. The white light flashed each time Izzy said *blink*.

"I don't see this light during the day," Sitara said.

"Most lighthouses shine all the time, but the North Light has a sun switch that measures the amount of light. It only goes on when it's dark enough—usually right before sunset." Izzy settled back. "I know all about the North Light because my mom's restaurant isn't far from there . . . it's in New Harbor."

"Your mother lives on that island," Sitara said. "My father told me."

"She doesn't live there. She's working there for the summer to help her family run their restaurant. She's coming home any day now," Izzy said. "My mom's a really good cook."

"My mother is too. Maybe she'll have a restaurant someday too."

"Maybe." Izzy nodded. "Your closet is like the one in

the book *The Lion, the Witch and the Wardrobe*," she said, remembering the story her mother used to read to her before bed. She smiled. "If only Mr. Tumnus were here."

"I don't know that story," Sitara said.

"It's really good. These kids travel to this magical place called Narnia."

"That sounds nice," Sitara said.

Izzy let her gaze follow the harbormaster's boat on its slow patrol. Besides him, the pond was silent.

"On summer nights in my village in Khost, when it was too hot or I wanted to be alone, I would go on our balcony." Sitara leaned back and stared into the sky. "There aren't as many stars here as at home— and they aren't as bright, but still, it's the same sky." She pointed at the sliver of a moon. "When the moon is brand-new like this, my mother tells me to make a dua. It means make a wish."

"Oh, I always wish on a falling star," Izzy said.

"Falling star?"

"You know, when you see a star race across the sky, you make a wish. Watch. There aren't many right now, but maybe we'll see one."

"Ah, yes, of course," Sitara said. "You know, my name means star in Dari."

"Really? What a cool name," Izzy said. "I wish my name was something about the ocean—Oceania or—"

"Seaweed."

Izzy glanced at Sitara, not knowing if she was kidding. Then Sitara giggled and Izzy couldn't help but laugh too. "No, not seaweed!"

At that moment, high above the world and hidden inside the night, Izzy suddenly felt brave. She stood, steadying herself against the chimney. "I am Amphitrite," she said. "The goddess queen of the sea!" She lifted a fist in the air. *If only I had a Wonder Woman cape*, she thought. The image made her laugh even louder.

Sitara clapped as Izzy took a bow.

"Hey, that star is falling!" Sitara said.

Izzy spun around in time to see the tail end, then she sat back down next to Sitara, anxious to find another. The sky was mesmerizing—dark and distant. Like the ocean, it seemed to go on forever. Sitting on that roof, it suddenly felt as if anything was possible.

"Do you know the constellations? I only know how to find the Big Dipper. See, it's there." Izzy pointed. "Oh, and Cassiopeia, there—it looks like a big W."

"I see those stars in Afghanistan too," Sitara said. "But my favorite constellation is Soraya. It's a group of six stars, but it's a winter constellation, so we won't be able to see it until November."

"Soraya," Izzy repeated. She liked the way it sounded. "You know a lot about stars."

"Yes, some days I think I will be like Al-Sufi. He was a famous Persian astronomer. Many astronomers based their writings on his book, *The Book of Fixed Stars*. He wrote poems too."

"You want to be an astronomer?"

"Maybe. Or a lawyer."

"Or a lawyer-astronomer," Izzy said.

Sitara smiled. "Yes, that's what I will be."

"What will you do as a lawyer-astronomer?"

"If someone complains about the stars, I will sue them!"

"Maybe if a star falls on someone, you can sue the star," Izzy said.

Sitara laughed. "Yes. And you can be my assistant."

"No, not me. I'm going to be an oceanographic cartographer."

"What's that?"

"Someone who makes maps of the ocean. Right now I'm mapping the pond."

Sitara looked away and smiled.

"What?" Izzy said.

"You are a scientist of the ocean. That's nice."

Izzy shrugged.

"I am hoping my father will let me go with you on your boat again," Sitara said.

Izzy realized she'd been silly to get mad at Sitara for jumping into the skiff yesterday. She would have done the same thing.

"What's your wish?" Sitara asked Izzy.

"I don't know," Izzy lied. She didn't feel like explaining about keeping the Sea Stars together or why she kept the key to an empty house.

"My wish is to go home," Sitara said.

Izzy stared at Sitara's profile and realized their wishes were the same.

They sat in silence, waiting for another shooting star. Izzy felt her eyelids get heavy. She began to worry that

Sitara's parents were looking for them. She didn't need to get blamed all over again for being somewhere they weren't supposed to be. If her dad found out, he'd probably take her phone away for a week—for real this time.

"We better get going," Izzy said. She stood, feeling off-balance and dizzy. As she carefully stepped toward the trapdoor, her arms shot out as if she were walking a tightrope.

Sitara skipped around her as if the roof were her playground.

Izzy followed her down the ladder, jumping from the last rung. Back in Sitara's room, the bright light made her blink. When she regained her sight, she saw the closet door was still shut. Their secret was safe.

Sitara was all smiles. "It will be our . . . What is the name of the place in your book?"

Izzy put her hand on the doorknob. "Narnia," she said.

"Narnia," Sitara repeated as if the word itself had magical powers.

"Okay," Izzy said. "Thanks." She closed Sitara's door behind her. She was happy that the Haidarys were not in the kitchen as she left their apartment.

When Izzy was back in her own room, she realized she'd forgotten to get the science homework.

She stared at her ceiling, knowing Sitara was right above her. She wished she could tap Morse code or some other message that said—SOS! NEED HOME-WORK NOW!

That's when she saw something white dangling outside her window. Izzy walked over to it and removed her window screen.

It was a piece of paper, pierced with a hook.

Izzy stuck her head out the window. Above her, Sitara leaned out of her own window, holding the fishing pole that they'd given her earlier. Her hijab was off and her long black hair fell loose around her face.

Izzy removed the paper from the hook. It was the science sheet. She glanced back up, to say thank you, but before she could say a word, Sitara had reeled in the line and ducked back inside her room.

Izzy couldn't help but grin as she stared up at the empty window where Sitara had just been.

"Thank you," she whispered into the night air.

Chapter 10

On Friday, as Izzy and Sitara wound their way through the long hallways to their lockers, it seemed as if even more kids were starting to notice Sitara.

Izzy watched two girls pause to gawk as they walked past. A boy darted by, shouting, "Go home!"

Whenever kids stared or pointed or whispered, Izzy wished a hole would open up in the floor so she could disappear. But Sitara didn't seem to care. She walked through the hallway with her head held high, as if she'd gone to Shoreline Regional Middle her entire life.

When they entered the tech ed room that morning,

they found Zelda in front of the assignment board, arms crossed.

"What's wrong?" Izzy asked.

Zelda threw her arms in the air. "He changed it. I dressed special for today and he put me on graphics."

All week, Zelda and Piper had read the news, but that morning, next to ANCHOR, Mr. Cantor had written: MANCINI/HAIDARY.

Izzy's hands flew to her mouth, partly out of surprise and partly to keep from throwing up.

"I—I . . . can't do that," she said as the angry-ocean sound filled her ears.

Sitara and Piper joined them.

"What's wrong?" Sitara asked.

"I dressed to do the news today and Mr. Cantor put you guys in," Zelda said.

"Is there a problem here?" Mr. Cantor suddenly appeared, peering over the tops of his wire-rimmed glasses at the girls. His polka-dot bow tie was turquoise.

The ocean sound in Izzy's ears was becoming a tsunami. "I—I, um . . . I thought I was just going to do script today again . . . um . . . and I'm not ready to—" she began.

Mr. Cantor removed his glasses. "I thought I made it clear when you joined this class that you should be prepared to do every job."

Zelda linked arms with Piper. "We can do it, Mr. Cantor. We had planned to go today, anyway." She smoothed her dress with her free hand to prove it.

Izzy watched Mr. Cantor's gaze dart from her to Zelda and back. Izzy did her best to look sick.

Mr. Cantor sighed heavily. "I don't usually allow for substitutions, but it is the first week."

"Excuse me, Mr. Cantor."

Everyone turned to stare at Sitara.

"It's my assignment too. I can still be anchor," she said.

Zelda unlinked arms with Piper. "I said we would do it."

"But it's my name there," Sitara said. "I would like this opportunity to introduce myself to the school."

Zelda's mouth gaped open.

A slow smile spread across Mr. Cantor's face. "Yes," he finally said. "I quite agree." He reached over to the board and erased Izzy's name. "Bravo, Miss Haidary. You are a true newsperson."

Then he paused to stare hard at Izzy. "Miss Mancini. I'd advise you not to expect the same treatment again." He turned on his heel and headed into the control room. "Remember, your grade depends on it."

Izzy swallowed hard as she followed Zelda, Piper, and Nathaniel into the control room. She took a seat in the corner and peered out the window where Sitara sat alone at the anchor desk.

Mr. Cantor raised a hand in the air. "Five, four," he began. *Three, two, one.* He pointed at Roger. The camera light turned green.

"Salâm alaykom. My name is Sitara Haidary and today is Friday, September seventh." Her voice was clear and smooth. Her hijab perfectly framed her face. Izzy thought it gave her a look of authority.

"Today is National Acorn Squash day. For lunch there is hot dog on a bun. Congratulations to the boys' soccer team for winning yesterday's game. On this day in history, in 1670, Governor Winthrop announced the foundation of the City of Boston, Massachusetts."

Sitara took a deep breath and stared intently into the camera. "My name is Sitara Haidary."

"Duh, we already know that," Zelda whispered a little too loudly.

"And I'm from Afghanistan. I am a Muslim and that is why I wear this headscarf." She touched her head. "It is called hijab." Roger zoomed in on Sitara's face.

"No one makes me wear hijab. It is my choice. It is part of my religion, and I wear it to show modesty. I am proud to wear it."

Izzy leaned forward in her seat. The studio seemed to dissolve around Sitara's words. Izzy was shocked she would talk about something so private in front of the entire school. She thought back to when Apollo was rude to Sitara on the bus. No matter what people said, no matter how they acted, Sitara didn't change who she was to make them stop. She just kept being Sitara.

"Instead of pointing or whispering, if you have any questions about hijab, it is okay to ask me. I like to talk about it. Thank you for listening. My name is Sitara Haidary and this is the Shoreline Regional Middle School news."

Music played as Mr. Cantor pointed at Roger. The camera went dark.

"That's a wrap," Mr. Cantor said. He walked over

to Sitara. "Well done, Miss Haidary," he said. "Well done."

Izzy glanced at Zelda to see what she thought about Sitara's speech. Zelda met her gaze with narrowed eyes and shook her head. Then she turned away.

Izzy shifted uncomfortably in her seat. Even though she hadn't said one word, Zelda's look told an entire story. Sitara might have been the one who took Zelda's place on TV, but Izzy was the one she blamed.

Izzy couldn't get Zelda's angry image out of her head all day. So, when the last class before lunch ended, she went straight to the cafeteria.

She felt bad for not waiting for Sitara at their lockers, but she needed to be alone with Zelda and Piper. Nothing had been the same since Sitara had shown up. If it could be just the three of them, eating lunch together like they had done forever, maybe things could go back to the way they were. They were the Sea Stars, after all. Best friends forever.

As Izzy stepped into the cafeteria, chaos seemed to press against her from every side. The tables were packed and a jumble of voices blended into a dull roar. The smell of disinfectant mixed with hot dog made her want to gag. Kids hopped in and out of a lunch line that snaked around the entire room.

"Find a seat, honey. You can't stand there," a lunch aide said.

The familiar angry-ocean sound began to fill her head.

"Hey!"

She spun around to see Piper.

"Come on, Zelda's saving seats."

Relief washed over Izzy. She followed Piper, and slid in across from Zelda.

"I'm so glad I found you guys," she said.

Zelda had already been through the line. A hot dog sat untouched on her tray as she nibbled on potato chips.

Izzy was having a hard time measuring her mood.

"Sleepover tomorrow!" Piper squeaked. "I can't wait! My mom even said I could miss piano so I can get there at a normal time."

Izzy's head popped up. "Sleepover?"

"Duh, Izzy, our Sea Star tradition!" Piper grinned. "Sleeping over at the marina is going to be so cool! Let's stay up all night! Can we go on the pond when it's dark?"

Zelda wrinkled her nose. "After you got sick last

time? No way. Plus it's buggy enough during the day. We'll get eaten alive at night." She gave Izzy a hard stare. "It's just the three of us, right?" she said. "We don't need any international guests."

"I found this new YouTube prank-guy that I have to show you. His videos are hi-lar-i-ous." Piper emphasized each syllable. "I was laughing so hard."

Izzy thought back to the afternoon they'd met at Sea Star Headquarters, the day before school began. She hadn't said no to the sleepover then, because Mom was supposed to be home. How would she explain why her mom wasn't there? What if Dad slipped into one of his moods? Or if Starenka tried to feed everyone cabbage or fell into one of her olden-days rants about how she could never have friends over because of all the cows she had to milk? And then there was the Sitara issue. There was no way her dad would let her have a sleepover without inviting Sitara. Never mind the fact that she was supposed to be visiting her mom Saturday on Block Island.

"Izzy?" Piper said. They were both staring at her.

"I'm sorry, you guys. I forgot I can't do the sleepover because . . . um . . . we're going to be on Block Island."

Piper looked as if someone had just told her that her puppy died. "You are?" she said. "You didn't tell me that."

"My father just let me know." Izzy said. *Which is true, technically*, she thought.

"Can we still come over on Sunday at least?" Piper asked. "My mom keeps asking when she can bring your mom the PTO stuff."

"My . . . um . . . mom says she can't do PTO after all."

"Oh," Piper said. "Well, *we* could still come over."

Izzy stared blankly at Piper, then Zelda.

Even though she knew she'd be home late on Saturday night, all of the other issues still existed—especially the fact that Mom still wouldn't be there. *How am I supposed to explain something I don't even understand?* she thought.

"Um, well, actually, we're going to spend the whole weekend on the island—Sunday too." Izzy stared at her peanut butter and Fluff sandwich. "My dad . . . um . . . my parents say I have to go."

"So, your mom just got home from Block Island and now you're all going back overnight? Where are you staying?" Zelda asked. Her eyes seemed to bore into Izzy like lasers.

"Um, I don't know. With the Aunts, I guess."

"I thought you said their cottage was too tiny for everyone to fit."

Izzy shrugged as she took a bite of her sandwich. It tasted like sand.

Zelda shook her head. "I can't believe you're ruining our back-to-school-sleepover streak."

Izzy swallowed hard.

"Her parents are making her go, Zelda," Piper said. "What's she supposed to do?"

But Zelda eyed her suspiciously. "You're sure this isn't about you-know-who?"

Just then, they all looked up to see Sitara standing in the middle of the cafeteria where Izzy had been only a moment ago. *She's looking for me*, Izzy thought. *I should get her.*

But Izzy's feet wouldn't budge.

Right then, Apollo moved behind Sitara. Izzy watched in horror as he reached up as if he was going to grab her hijab. Zelda covered her mouth but let a giggle escape.

Fortunately, Sitara was so busy searching for a place to sit, she didn't seem to notice. Izzy waved, and

Sitara made a beeline to their table. Apollo threw his hands up and Zelda laughed harder.

"I used to hate Apollo when we were in second grade," Zelda said. "But he's gotten really cute all of a sudden."

"Ewww," Piper said. "He's gross. And mean."

Zelda smiled. "Not really if you get to know him."

"Stop, Zelda," Piper said, putting her hand up. "That is so . . . ick."

Sitara slipped into the seat next to Izzy. She looked around the table. "I'm very happy to find you. It's so noisy in here."

Zelda sipped from her water bottle as she watched Sitara pull containers from a bag. The spicy smell of last night's feast flooded the table.

Zelda wrinkled her nose. "What is that?" she asked.

"It's qabuli palaw," Sitara said. "Izzy and I had it for dinner last night."

Zelda's gaze shifted to Izzy. "So you guys eat together now too?" Her voice dripped with accusation.

"Only last night," Izzy said.

Zelda faced Sitara. "You shouldn't eat that."

"Why not?" Sitara asked.

Izzy started to get a sick feeling in her stomach.

"Because." Zelda pushed her lunch tray toward her. "You're in America. You should eat American food. Like a hot dog."

Izzy froze. She knew the Haidarys had strict rules about what they ate. She thought back to the lobster dinner that ended up being corn and potatoes. Starenka had said it was because the lobster had looked strange to them. But Izzy's dad had later said that lobster was forbidden by their religion. *It's like us during Lent*, her father had said. *Lots of religions have food restrictions.*

"No, thank you," Sitara said.

"You know, Izzy," Piper said as she opened her yogurt. "I've been asking my mom all summer if we could go to Block Island. Maybe we could go and hang out with you? Just for the day, I mean."

"Um, well . . . I don't know which ferry we're taking yet," Izzy said.

"Text me when you know," Piper said.

"Yeah, probably the early one. I know your mom likes to sleep in on weekends," Izzy said.

"She'll get up early for Block Island."

"But we're moving some of my mom's stuff home and . . . you know how the Aunts can be," she lied.

Piper stared hard at Izzy. "If you don't want me to go with you, Izzy, just say so."

"It's not that . . ." Izzy's words trailed off.

Piper stared at her yogurt.

Izzy turned to see if Zelda was going to ask about Block Island, too, but she didn't seem to be listening.

"Haven't you ever had a hot dog? They're really good. A Rhode Island specialty." She pushed the tray toward Sitara again.

Izzy's mouth tasted sour.

"No, thank you," Sitara repeated.

"What's wrong with it?" Zelda raised an eyebrow.

"She doesn't want it, Zelda." Izzy tried to make eye contact with Piper. *I could use your help here*, she was trying to say with her eyes. But Piper was still staring at her uneaten yogurt.

"I can only eat food that is halâl."

"Halâl? What's that?"

"Halâl means permissible. It is food that the Qur'ân says is okay to eat if you are Muslim. I am sorry, but this food is harâm for me. I cannot eat it. Thank you, though. Would you like to try some qabuli palaw?"

"No, thanks," Zelda said. "I only eat American food." The table got quiet. "Like hot dogs."

Izzy stared at her friend. *Why are you doing this?* she wanted to scream.

Zelda picked up her tray. "Never mind. I have to go to my locker before class."

"Oh, okay," Piper said as she put her uneaten yogurt away.

Izzy looked at the clock. "We still have eight minutes."

Zelda flashed a smile. "Got stuff . . . you know . . . to do." She got up and made a beeline toward the door. Piper stuck behind her as if they were tied together by an invisible rope.

"I'm sorry," Sitara said. "I didn't mean to hurt Zelda's feelings by not trying the hot dog."

Izzy stared at her half-eaten peanut butter sandwich. She thought about taking another bite, but didn't think it would go down.

"No . . ." Izzy shook her head. "She's just being, I don't know . . . weird."

Lunch used to be the best part of the day, Izzy thought. *But now it's become an uneaten sandwich and best friends who are slipping away.*

"I guess we might as well go too," she said.

154

Chapter 11

On Saturday morning, Izzy's father drove her to the Port of Galilee for the eight a.m. ferry to Block Island. It left from the same place his fishing boat, the *Isabella Rose*, was docked. Izzy wondered if he'd been back there since he'd decided to quit the fishing business. Her father had always loved fishing, and it had been a difficult time when he realized he couldn't do it professionally anymore.

They drove in silence, Izzy occasionally glancing at his stern profile. A year ago—before Afghanistan—he would have been all smiles and jokes. But on that day, he gripped the steering wheel with white knuckles and his mouth remained a tight line.

When they were at the ferry, her father pulled over to the curb. Izzy already had her ticket so she could go straight aboard. The sharp smells of fish and ocean filled the cab, and for a moment it all seemed so familiar—as if they were there to clean the boat or take it out for what she used to call a putt-putt cruise when she was little. It didn't seem that long ago when she would have bounded out of the truck, racing down the pier to the *Isabella Rose*.

But on that day, she remained in the truck's cab, hugging her patchwork bag to her chest and trying to ignore the angry-ocean sound that kept reminding her that no matter how tightly she tried to hold on to things, her world seemed to be slipping away.

"I'll be waiting right here when you get back at nine tonight," he said. "Are you sure you're okay by yourself?"

"I'm fine, Dad." She leaned over to give him a peck on the cheek, then slipped out of the cab, quickly falling into the crowd of tourists wheeling suitcases and bicycles up the gangplank. It was a good sign that it was the *Carol Jean*. It was her favorite of all the Block Island ferries.

Izzy wanted to be excited. Boarding the ferry was always a festive event. Toddlers rode high on their fathers' shoulders, kids pulled on their mothers' arms, teens rolled their bikes aboard. Tourists snacked on saltwater taffy and fudge. The scent of sunscreen was everywhere. Since it was the Saturday after Labor Day, the line was filled with runners heading over for the annual Run Around the Block.

But instead of cheering her up, all of these little details seemed to only remind her of what was missing.

As she made her way up the gangplank, she saw her dad's friend Matt collecting tickets.

"Heading to the island like a tourist?" he scoffed. "What's your old man up to?"

"He dropped me off." Izzy shrugged, trying to hide the catch in her throat. "Too much work at the marina."

Matt laughed and shook his head. "Don't know what he's thinkin'. Running a marina is like running a circus." He cocked his head. "Your mom's not still working at Loretta's, is she? I thought that was only for the summer."

"She'll be home soon," Izzy said. "Definitely this week." She handed him her ticket and dashed off before he could ask another question.

She took the stairs two at a time, until she was on the top observation deck. A pile of twisted rope as thick as her arm was rolled up in the corner. Izzy stepped around it so she could lean over the starboard side. She scanned the docks until she found the *Isabella Rose*, bobbing in her slip. Seaweed still clung to her nets and rust stained her hull.

The *Carol Jean* blew a loud, long blast of its horn, and Izzy nearly jumped out of her shoes. *Gets me every time*, she thought. But that was okay. That sound signaled the beginning of all things good—salty air, ocean spray, and right then, Mom.

The ferry rolled out of port. Fishermen, lining the boulders that formed the breakwall, paused to wave as the *Carol Jean* passed by on her way out to sea. The farther they coasted from the mainland, the lighter Izzy began to feel. The fishy smells from the docks disappeared and she inhaled the clear ocean air. She stared into the green late-summer waves of the Atlantic. *The cure for everything is salt water*, her mom always said. Izzy felt a tinge of excitement. She'd be with Mom soon and that was as good a cure as salt water.

As they entered the Atlantic, the ferry rolled with the waves. Izzy let her gaze drift down the coast. Out of habit she named the beaches—East Matunuck, Deep Hole, Matunuck, Moonstone, Green Hill, Brogee's, Charlestown . . . until the rest disappeared in the haze. Oceanside Pond and the marina were set too far back, but in her mind's eye she could still see her dad moving up and down the docks and Dr. Haidary elbow-deep in an engine.

The coast grew fainter and fainter until it disappeared, and the ferry was surrounded by ocean as far as the eye could see. As she looked across the horizon, a lonely, hollow feeling washed over her. Suddenly she felt abandoned. Angry, even. *Why am I traveling to Block Island?* she wondered. *Mom promised she'd be home by now. And what is Dad doing about it? He just made things worse by letting the Haidarys move upstairs.*

Izzy wanted to spit her worries into the never-ending waves that rolled on and on. Instead, she stuffed her feelings into a stifled sob. Then, when she didn't think she could feel any lonelier, Block Island materialized out of the fog.

"Fine day for a trip to the island."

Izzy turned to see the captain on his way to the stern, where he would steer the ferry into port.

"Where's your dad?" he asked. "Can't tear himself away from his marina?" He shook his head. "I been meaning to stop over. Sure miss seeing him at the docks."

Izzy nodded.

Moments later, the *Carol Jean* pulled into Old Harbor. Izzy scurried down the stairs, positioning herself so that she could be the first passenger off after the cars exited.

When the last one left the ramp, she rushed down the gangplank. She could hear a band tuning up at Ballard's Beach. The smell of clam cakes wafted in the air. Tourists walked by sipping Del's lemonade. Summer might have ended on the mainland, but it was in full swing on Block Island.

"Izzy! Izzy!" Mom stood in front of her wearing cut-off jean shorts and a flannel shirt. She was tanner and thinner than when Izzy had last seen her. She wore a floppy yellow hat and carried a beach bag.

"Mom!" Izzy ran to her, wrapping her arms around her.

"I'm so sorry I missed the first day of school, honey," she said.

"It's okay."

"Well, I'm going to make it up to you today. Come on! I packed lunch. Do you want to go for a swim at Mansion Beach or look for sea glass at Sandy Point?"

"You don't have to work?"

"Vera and Loretta are covering for me so I can spend the day with you."

"Really?" Izzy couldn't contain her grin.

Mom nodded.

"Sandy Point. Definitely." She cocked her head. "You know I don't swim in the ocean, Mom."

"You used to love the ocean, Iz. I thought maybe you'd gotten over that."

Izzy shook her head. "Sandy Point."

"Well, come on then, let's go."

Izzy followed Mom to the parking lot. "Can we check out the North Light while we're there?"

"Of course. And later, I'll show you all the work I've done at the restaurant. You'll hardly recognize the place . . . and I have a surprise for you." They walked up to a white Jeep with no roof or doors. "Ta-da!"

"No way! Whose is it?"

"Mine," Mom said. "I needed something to get around the island. It's got a lot of miles on it, but it runs. Isn't it perfect?"

"Are you bringing it home?"

Mom shrugged, turning away. "Come on, let's go have fun!"

As they turned onto Corn Neck Road, Izzy's hair whipped in the wind. The sun had burned off the haze. Izzy closed her eyes, letting the warm breeze wrap around her like a hug. When the road ended, Mom parked the Jeep at the Block Island National Wildlife Refuge and jumped out, grabbing a blanket and a large basket from the back. "Ready?" she said.

They followed the dirt path toward the North Light. Seagulls circled above them, cawing as if they had

X-ray vision, which let them see inside Mom's basket at all the yummy stuff she'd packed.

Izzy paused to take in the lighthouse. It felt weird to be standing so close to it instead of searching for it on the horizon. Since it was daytime, the lighthouse stood dark and stoic, as if calmly waiting for dusk, when it would spring into action.

"I've always thought there was something holy about the North Light," Mom said.

"It looks like a church," Izzy said, scanning its granite, gray stones, and white tower. "Whenever I see the North Light's beam, I think of you, Mom. I don't know . . . knowing it's on watch all night makes me feel safe."

Mom reached out to grab Izzy's hand. "I love that you think that, Izzy-bug," she said. "You know I'm always thinking of you."

The northernmost tip of the island pointed directly at Brogee's Beach. When they walked to the very end, Mom took a deep breath. "Block Island is the Bermuda of New England," she said.

Izzy loved the spot because it was the only place she knew of where the Atlantic Ocean met itself. The current and wind and tide on either side of the island converged at that point so that the waves crashed into each other in what seemed like an endless ocean collision. Izzy had been there before with Mom and Dad during a stormy high tide, when the spray reached well over even Dad's head. It reminded Izzy of the way the pond met the ocean inside the breachway.

Mom spread out the blanket and began unpacking food. Izzy plopped down, her stomach growling. But instead of food, Mom handed her a small box wrapped in blue paper. "First, a present," she said.

Izzy grinned. "What for?"

Mom shrugged. "For fun. Open it."

Izzy peeled off the wrapping paper and opened the box. Inside was a tiny silver sea star attached to a piece of blue sea glass.

"I love it!"

"Let me put it around your neck."

"Thank you, Mom." Izzy touched a finger to the delicate charm. "I'm going to wear it every day."

Mom smiled. "Now food. I've got all of your favorites—spinach pie and pizza strips and some of Loretta's cookies."

The day couldn't get more perfect.

After eating at least two of everything, and at least four of the cookies, Izzy leaned back on her elbows. "I haven't been this full since the Haidarys made us dinner."

"I'm sorry I haven't met them yet," Mom said.

Izzy wanted to point out that she would have met them if she'd come home on Labor Day like she was supposed to, but she didn't want to ruin the day.

"They have a daughter your age, right? What's her name again?" Mom asked.

"Sitara," Izzy said.

"Sitara. That's such a pretty name. It must be nice having a friend at the marina. Is she adjusting to the middle school?"

Izzy shielded her eyes from the sun. "She's okay." Izzy was beginning to get annoyed at how her parents seemed more concerned about Sitara than her. She sat up and dug her heel into the soft sand. "Did you know they were coming?"

"Yes. Dad called to ask if he could move my things into the mechanics' workshop."

"Aren't you mad? You hate Afghanistan and now

165

it's like ... I don't know ... like it's living with us. Dad definitely talks about it more."

Mom stared into the water. "I don't hate Afghanistan, Izzy. I hate the war. I hate what it did to Dad. What it did to us."

Izzy turned away. It was the first time she'd heard Mom blame the war and Dad's military service for how everything seemed to be changing. Izzy realized she'd probably been thinking it for a long time, but had never said it because Dad got really upset if anyone said anything bad against the army.

It's like her mother's words had been there all along, floating just below the surface. But by saying them out loud, Izzy felt as if Mom had unpacked all the bad stuff the same as she'd unpacked the food from the picnic basket. Now her words lay across the blanket where Izzy had to look at them. She didn't like that at all.

Izzy turned away. "Dad's better now, Mom. He doesn't get angry like he used to, and he seems to really like the marina. He works real hard and—"

Mom put her arm around Izzy. "I know, Izzy. Dad's amazing. You don't have to tell me that." She looked her straight in the eye. "That's not why I'm still here, you know."

"Then why *are* you still here?"

Mom stared across the harbor toward Brogee's. "I'm figuring that out."

Izzy bit the inside of her cheek to keep from crying. She had wanted to keep the day light and fun. She didn't want to be talking about any of this.

After a moment, Mom asked, "Has Sitara fit in with the Sea Stars?"

Izzy rolled her eyes. She was glad to change the subject—but not to that subject. "She's met them."

Mom must have read her tone because she said, "Good?"

"Not really."

"Why not?"

Izzy dug her heel into the soft sand. "I don't know. Sitara changes everything." Izzy sighed. "It's weird."

"Well, I'm sure you're doing everything to make her feel welcome."

Izzy started to get angry. Why was Sitara her responsibility?

"I don't understand why she has to wear long-sleeved

everything and that headscarf all the time. It would be a lot easier for her if she tried to fit in."

Her mom smiled. "Izzy, that's her culture . . . and her religion. It would be like . . . I don't know, if you went to Afghanistan and you had to dress like she does. You'd feel more comfortable in your own clothes, right?"

"But why does she have to wear it *all* the time?"

"Why don't you ask her?" Mom said. "Are kids giving her a hard time?"

Izzy shrugged.

"Well, make sure you stick up for her."

Izzy began to fume. "I feel bad sometimes, okay—the way kids stare and whisper and point. But what am I supposed to do?"

"Feeling bad when someone's being treated poorly is fine and all, Izzy, but until you actually do something to change things . . . well, what's the point?"

"I can't make everyone like her."

"Zelda and Piper have been your friends for a long time. If you welcome Sitara into the group, they will too."

Izzy thought about Zelda and how she had acted

when Sitara wouldn't give up her turn to do the news and wouldn't try the hot dog. She wasn't sure if that was true.

Right then, thinking about Sitara and Piper and Zelda was like staring at the colliding waves in front of her. It was as if Sitara was coming in from the left and the Sea Stars were coming in from the right and their worlds were meeting in a giant crash of water. Making Zelda include Sitara in the Sea Stars seemed as likely as making the ocean change direction.

Izzy stood and walked as close to the water as she could without getting wet. She stared across the sound at Brogee's Beach—where she usually stood and looked at Block Island. Somehow, being on the other side of the water made everything feel backward and upside down.

The waves grew as the tide rolled in—meeting with such force that their spray shot several feet into the air. Suddenly her mother was behind her. "It must be getting high tide," she said.

Crash, the water sprayed.

"The ocean is getting angry," Izzy said.

"Oh, I don't see it as anger," Mom said. "It's energy. Can't you feel it? Close your eyes and listen."

Izzy shut her eyes, listening to the rush of water. There was a rhythm to it—first the tide pulling the sand and shells and tiny stones back, and then the swell as the water curved into a wave. Then the crash—a collision of water, sending out a million particles of ocean that dotted Izzy's hair and face and entered her nose and mouth, leaving a salty taste on her lips.

Even as she stood on the beach, she could feel the ocean's energy pulsing beneath its surface. For a second, she remembered back to when she was little, before Deep Hole, back before she'd become afraid of the ocean. She had loved the waves then. She had loved that energy.

Izzy opened her eyes and watched the ocean curve and swell into another giant wave, but this time when it crashed against the shore, she let its cold water wash over her feet.

Mom put her arm around Izzy. "Ready for that walk?" she asked.

Izzy nodded.

They headed down the beach, scouring the sand for

bits of shiny color. They each found a piece of green sea glass and Izzy found a blue one, which was extra-special rare. When they finally turned to make their way back to the blanket, the sun was low in the sky— another reminder that summer would be ending soon.

"How about an early supper at the restaurant, and I'll have you back on the ferry by seven forty-five?" Mom said.

"Seven *fifty*-five," Izzy said. "I already have my ticket."

After a breezy Jeep ride to New Harbor, they came to Loretta's Kitchen.

Inside, Aunt Loretta and Aunt Vera swarmed about Izzy as if it had been years instead of months since they'd last seen her. They wouldn't stop commenting on how tall she'd gotten and how pretty she'd become. Izzy couldn't deny that the attention was kind of nice.

"The Aunts," as they called them, were really Izzy's great-aunts. She'd never seen them without their aprons, or a dusting of flour in their tight gray curls.

"Sit, Isabella," Loretta said. "You've gotten too skinny."

"Mangia!" Vera said. "You need some meat on your bones."

171

After her second bowl of tortellini, Izzy said to her mom, "I wish Starenka would learn to cook like this."

"Your grandmother is a good cook," Mom said.

"Yeah, if you like cabbage," Izzy replied.

Mom laughed. "That's her food, not quite the same as Italian, but still good."

When Izzy finally got the Aunts to stop feeding her, she helped bus tables. She liked watching her mom, who seemed to be everywhere at once—seating customers, delivering food, helping in the kitchen. There was something different about her on Block Island. Even though she was working really hard, she seemed to have more energy. It made it even harder for Izzy to think about leaving without her.

Suddenly Mom yelled, "Izzy! It's seven forty. We need to go! Your father will kill me if you miss the last ferry."

"I could always stay and work here." Izzy let the idea hang in the air.

"I can see that." Mom grabbed her keys as the Aunts bagged food for Izzy to bring home. She hugged them both, then climbed into the Jeep.

It was thrilling, racing to the ferry. Izzy hoped

they'd missed it, but when they got to Old Harbor, the *Anna C.* was waiting.

"Whew," Mom said. "Just in time. You ready?"

"Not yet. They're still loading cars." Even though she felt guilty about keeping her mom away from the restaurant, she wanted to stay with her as long as possible.

"Okay." Mom cut the engine.

"The restaurant sure is busy," Izzy finally said. "Loretta and Vera are going to miss you when you're gone."

Mom nodded slowly. "Business has started to drop off now that most of the tourists have left, but I'm creating a winter menu with takeout options for the residents."

"Winter menu?" Izzy asked. "For what? Loretta's closes after Columbus Day."

Izzy's mom was quiet.

"Right?" Izzy said.

"Well," Mom began. "We're thinking of keeping it open."

"We?" Izzy sat up straight. "Why would the Aunts do that? They didn't want to open at all this summer and they know you're leaving."

173

"Actually, Izzy, it was my idea."

"What do you mean?"

Mom shook her head. "I . . . I need a little more time."

The angry-ocean sound began to swell.

"More time for what?"

Mom swallowed hard.

Izzy stared at the bag of food on her lap. She shifted her legs. "S-so—" She swallowed back a lump in her throat. "When *are* you coming home?"

Her mother looked out the Jeep's empty window frame. "Oh, honey, you know I'm only a boat ride a—"

"You're not a boat ride away. You might as well be a million miles away. I can't see you whenever I want—there are ferry schedules and school schedules and—"

Mom reached for Izzy, but she shrugged off her hug. She hated feeling selfish. But the day had reminded her how much she missed her mother.

"Remember a few years ago when we took a walk on Brogee's and there were all those starfish that had washed up onshore?" Mom said.

Mom was starting to sound like Starenka with her olden-days stories popping out of nowhere.

"They're sea stars, Mom."

"Sea stars! My scientist." Mom leaned over and kissed Izzy on the head. "Do you remember?"

"I don't know . . . yeah . . . what's that got to do with anything?"

Mom leaned back, looking at the darkening sky. "I was just thinking about it because I remember how no one said anything—but then all of a sudden the three of us started gathering sea stars at the same time and placing them back in the tide." Mom turned to Izzy. "Do you know why?"

Maybe Mom thought that if she talked about a happy memory, it would make what she was telling Izzy not hurt as much. But it still hurt. A lot. And Izzy wasn't going to play along and pretend it didn't.

"They're done loading cars. I have to go," she said as she slipped out of the Jeep and started running for the ferry.

"Wait! Izzy!" her mom called after her.

But Izzy didn't stop. Instead, she ran onto the gangplank and stormed up the steps. On the third-floor observation deck, she moved to the stern, scanning the parking lot.

She found her mom immediately—standing outside the Jeep, waving her arms and blowing kisses.

The ferry's horn gave its long, loud blast, and Mom jumped.

Izzy wanted to smile. She wanted to yell, *It always gets me too!* But the one thing she didn't want to do was wave back.

She pressed her new sea star necklace against her heart and stood, stone-still, as the *Anna C.* pulled out of Old Harbor.

As the ferry chugged farther and farther away, her mom got smaller and smaller until she disappeared altogether. When they entered the ocean, Izzy looked over the port side to find the North Light, its lens now lit.

"Blink . . . one . . . two . . . three . . . four . . . blink," she said slowly. On each *blink* the white light sent its signal into the night. *Careful! Warning! Look out!*

Right then, Izzy couldn't help but think back to that day on Brogee's Beach—back when she could still save the things she loved.

Third Grade

It was the kind of September day when you'd swear it was still July.

The sky was a deep, bright blue, and it matched the ocean so closely, you couldn't tell where the sky ended and the water began.

Mom said all we needed was palm trees and you'd think we were in Bermuda.

Dad had just gotten a job working on the fishing boat SarahBeth *and he was about to set off for an off-shore trip that would keep him away for over a week. His truck was packed with his bag and he and Mom stood hugging on the front lawn. I ran over and joined in. Mom and I pretended we weren't going to let him go.*

"One more walk on the beach," I begged. "Please! Just to Brogee's and back."

Dad looked at his watch. "I guess we can go down and back. But we have to go quick."

Flotsam barked and pranced in the air as we headed down Rosewood Avenue to Surfside. The parking lot gate was lowered, so we walked around.

I remember there had been a storm the day before, and there was red seaweed and shells scattered across the beach. But that was no surprise—the beach was constantly changing. Each day, you never knew what you'd find.

When we reached the Sea Star Headquarters, I saw them first. Hundreds of tiny sea stars were scattered across the beach.

I stared up at that cloudless sky that had seemed like a gift only a moment ago, but now seemed like a villain as the full sun beat down on those tiny lifeless creatures stuck in the hot sand.

Without a word spoken—and at the exact same second—we each jumped into action.

Mom held out her shirttail and began to gather sea stars in it, then placed them in the water so they could gently float away.

Dad was right behind her, a row of sea stars down his arm.

I ran over and gently picked one up. The tiny star seemed to pulse in my hand, like a baby's heart.

"It's okay, little sea star," I said. "I'm taking you home. Your mama's waiting. Here you go."

I lowered it into the ocean.

The three of us ran back and forth between the beach and the water. Carefully, gently, until the beach was empty.

At first, the sea stars seemed to just float there, on the water's surface.

Then they were gone.

"Are they going to be okay?" I asked.

Mom and Dad each put an arm around me.

"Yes," Dad said. "I'm sure of it."

"You saved the starfish, Izzy-bug. You are a true friend of the ocean."

"They're sea stars, Mom," I said, rolling my eyes, and Mom and Dad started laughing.

We ran back to the house and jumped in the truck. Mom sped all the way to Galilee, honking when we got to the docks.

The SarahBeth was about to leave.

Dad leapt onto the ship and the captain barked so loudly at him that I could hear everything.

He had said that if Dad didn't want the job, he'd find someone else who did.

But Dad didn't care. I watched him pulling in the bumpers and stowing the dock lines as they headed out of the harbor.

Before they were out of sight, I heard him shout, "We saved the sea stars, Izzy!"

And as loud as I could I yelled back, "Hey, Dad! Yes, we did!"

Chapter 12

The next morning, Izzy woke to an empty apartment.

She peeked inside Starenka's room. Her bed was made—straight and tight. Izzy knew she must be at mass. Normally, her grandmother would have brought Izzy with her, but she probably let her sleep in because she got home so late. Izzy didn't mind going to mass, but she liked sleeping in too.

Izzy padded into the kitchen, looking for her dad. The sun was up and it seemed like a perfect day for measuring. But for the data to be consistent, she had to wait for mean low tide. Dad would know exactly when that was.

She headed downstairs. When she reached the lure display in the middle of the shop, she heard voices coming from her father's office. She froze midstep.

"We've already been through so much." It was Dr. Haidary's voice. "I used to think that someday we would be able to go home and be reunited with our family—my parents and my brothers. Now this."

Izzy knew she probably shouldn't be listening, but she was curious too. She ducked behind the display so they wouldn't see her if they came out.

"I'm so sorry, Hassan. Is there a lot of damage?"

"My brother emailed me photos. Our home . . . it's ruined." Dr. Haidary's voice cracked. "They ransacked it and then set it on fire."

"Hassan, I am so sorry," her father said. There was a pause. "Do the kids know?"

"No, but I cannot hide it from them forever," he said. "The boys are still young. They don't really understand, but Sitara is wise. She understands everything—too much for her age. I am afraid this news will destroy her."

"Sitara is stronger than you think," Dad said.

"She is strong but she hides her pain too."

"I know what you mean," Dad said. "The war . . . when I came home, no one could understand what I'd been through. It changes a person. At first, I didn't want to talk about it." He sighed. "But eventually I realized I needed to—not only for me, but for Angela and Izzy." Her father took a deep breath. "If only I could have changed things sooner."

"That's what I mean," Dr. Haidary said. "Sitara's scars are on the inside. She hides them from the world. But what's worse, I think, is that she hides them from herself."

"You need to let her find her own way too, Hassan. Give her some freedom. Let her make her own choices. I think it will help her deal with what happened at home."

There was a pause, then Dr. Haidary's voice got louder. Izzy could tell they had moved into the middle of the shop.

"I did not want to let her do the news class at school, but you talked me into that," he said.

"Yes, and that's been great," Dad said. "The more

183

new things she tries, the better. You know we're here for you, Hassan. Whatever we can do to help."

Izzy peeked around the display, watching their backs as they headed for the screen door. She decided to wait until they were in the workshop before running out to ask him.

"Hi, Izzy. What are you doing?"

Izzy almost jumped out of her skin. She turned to see Sitara standing behind her. Izzy's father and Dr. Haidary spun around.

"How long have you two been there?" Dad asked.

"I came down the stairs just now," Sitara said.

Izzy looked up sheepishly.

"Hmmm," her father said.

"I was trying to find out when it will be mean low tide," Izzy said.

Her father glanced at his watch. "In about an hour, but you can start taking soundings now. Why don't you both go?"

"Really?" Izzy asked.

At the mention of the boat, Sitara seemed to stand taller.

Dr. Haidary looked at Izzy's father as if he had two heads. "This is not a good idea, Vince," he said.

"It's fine, Hassan," Izzy's dad said. "Outside the channel, the water will barely reach her waist. Plus, both girls will wear a life jacket at all times. Right, Izzy?"

Izzy nodded reluctantly.

Dr. Haidary looked away. Izzy wondered if he was thinking about what her father had said earlier. *Give her some freedom.*

"Please, Baba. I want to go! I will be very careful," Sitara said.

"You will go slowly and stay where it is shallow?"

Izzy nodded. "Yes—yes, Dr. Haidary. We will be safe. I promise."

"Izzy is a certified boat operator," her father said, winking. "It will be good for them, Hassan."

Dr. Haidary's mouth was a straight line. He finally nodded. "Okay. But not too long."

Sitara jumped up and down, clapping. "Yes, Baba!" she said.

"Let me get my bag and sounding stuff," Izzy said

before anyone changed their mind. "I'll meet you at the dock."

Flotsam and Sitara were waiting by the skiff when Izzy returned.

"First I have to get you a life jacket." Izzy hopped onto the boat and lifted the seat. She pulled out two orange vests. She helped Sitara put hers on before she put on her own.

Izzy climbed back into the skiff and reached for Sitara. "Take my hand and step into the middle," she said.

But before Sitara could get into the boat, Flotsam jumped in front of her, sending it rocking. Sitara worked to regain her balance as Flotsam scrambled to his place on the bow.

"Oh no, Flotsam." Izzy moved to the bow and tugged on his collar, but he wouldn't budge.

"Let him come," Sitara said. "It will be fun."

Izzy shook her head at Flotsam, who gave his sorry-not-sorry look. Izzy guided Sitara into her seat on the bench in front, just behind Flotsam. Izzy moved to the stern so she could navigate.

When everyone was settled, Izzy said, "Ready?"

Sitara squeaked out a giggle. "I'm ready!" she shouted.

Izzy pulled the cord and gave the throttle a quick twist. The engine rumbled awake, kicking up silt. She hit reverse and backed out of the slip, turning before slowly navigating around and past the fuel dock. She was surprised how nervous she felt with Sitara aboard.

Red right return, she reminded herself, making sure she kept the skiff between the green buoys on the right and red buoys on the left.

A large Grady-White barreled down the dredged channel that larger boats used to access the Atlantic. The captain waved an apology as the skiff rocked up and down in its wake. Sitara clutched her bench.

"Are you okay?" Izzy yelled.

Sitara turned toward Izzy, her face flushed with excitement. Her hijab had fallen back, revealing her long black hair. "Yes!" she shouted. "Can you go faster?"

Izzy couldn't help but grin back. "After we pass the no wake sign." She knew how thrilling the boat could be. But seeing the excitement spark in Sitara's eyes made it even better.

She navigated around the oyster farm on the right and the sunken barge on the left. The ocean air rushed about them. Salty drops of water dotted their faces and clothes. Sitara's loose scarf flapped in the breeze.

Izzy had been used to circumventing clammers and kayakers and stand-up paddlers for most of the summer, but on that September day, the pond belonged to them.

As they passed the last NO WAKE sign, Izzy threw the engine into high. Sitara squealed. Her scarf flapped about her head, looking like a kite about to take off.

The breachway churned and gurgled in front of them. Izzy kept her distance. She had already measured this spot and knew it got shallow quickly. If she wasn't careful, she'd ground the boat, or even worse, dent a blade. She lifted the motor halfway out of the water.

"How are you able to drive this boat when you are too young to drive a car?" Sitara asked.

"In Rhode Island there is no minimum age to get your operator's license. You have to go to Providence and take a test from DEM. I passed on the first try, and they sent me my license in the mail. I've been able to drive a boat since I was ten."

"You're very lucky," Sitara said. "In Afghanistan, most women cannot drive a car. My mother can't."

"Why not?"

Sitara shrugged. "It's different for women there." She pointed. "What's that bird? It looks as graceful as a ballet dancer with its long legs and neck."

"It's a snowy egret," Izzy said.

"Her knees bend backward while her body moves forward. She is a very elegant bird, I think."

"They look like knees but those are actually her ankles. She is walking on her toes." Izzy had seen egrets her whole life, but somehow Sitara's description made her see that one differently. She cut the engine so they could float in silence.

Sitara squealed and pointed into the water, where it looked as if a blob of clear Jell-O was floating by. "What's that?" she asked.

"It's a jellyfish." Izzy grabbed a net and scooped it up for Sitara to see up close.

Sitara examined the jellyfish. "I've never seen anything like that."

"They don't look like most fish," Izzy said. "You have to be careful of them when you're in the water. They sting." She lowered the net so the jellyfish could float away. "How do you say fish in Pashto?"

"Mâhi," Sitara said.

"Mâhi," Izzy repeated. "That's funny. Sometimes my dad catches a fish called mahi-mahi."

Sitara peered over the side of the boat as a tiny crab scampered below.

"That's a hermit crab," Izzy said. She scooped him up and put him on the bench next to Sitara. He tucked himself into his shell.

Sitara leaned forward, examining the crab. "You are very smart," she told him. "You carry your home wherever you go."

Izzy gently placed the hermit crab back into the water, where he emerged from his shell and scrambled away.

"I am like this crab," Sitara said. "It was like I was picked up in one place, then dropped off somewhere else. And I had to carry my whole house on my back too."

Izzy couldn't help but think about what she had

overheard. She knew something bad had happened to Sitara's home in Afghanistan. She suddenly felt guilty knowing about it before Sitara did.

They floated by a sandbar, crammed with seagulls. "I call that spot Seagull Island. You can only see it at low tide; otherwise it's all under water."

"Mërghëy," Sitara said. "That is *bird* in Pashto. But I have never seen birds like that before. Look how they all face into the wind. They do not hide from it."

A seagull lifted its wings, and its body slowly rose until it seemed to float on air. Sitara sucked in her breath. "They are magic mërghëy, I think." She raised her own arms as if the breeze could lift her too.

Izzy laughed.

"Show me how you do the measuring for your maps," Sitara said.

"Sure," Izzy said. "The technical way to say it is that we're taking soundings. It's the term used when measuring the depth of a body of water." She navigated the skiff past Egret Point. "I was planning on doing Mack's Cove next."

When they reached the cove, Izzy cut the engine and tossed the anchor into the water with a splash.

Then she took out the clipboard that held her latest working map.

She showed Sitara her phone. "See this app? It shows me that the latitude here is 41.357951 and the longitude is −71.639947. I record these numbers here." Izzy made a dot and recorded the numbers. "Then I drop the weight, attached to its string exactly at that point."

Izzy let the five-ounce fishing lead fall into the water.

"Each knot on the string is six inches apart. I pinch it like this at the water's surface, then I pull it out and count the knots."

Izzy lifted the dripping string from the water and counted.

"About four feet. I mark that next to the GPS co-ordinates." She peeled seaweed off the weight and handed it to Sitara. "Do you want to try?" she asked.

Sitara nodded.

"Okay, so I move about ten feet closer to shore and mark that on my map." Izzy made another dot. "And do it all over again."

Making sure there was enough slack in the anchor line, Izzy restarted the engine and moved closer to the shore. She cut the motor and handed the weight to Sitara, who dropped it in, carefully pinching it at the surface. She counted the knots. "Seven knots, so that's three and a half feet," she said proudly.

"Perfect," Izzy said. "Usually I get out at this point to measure because it's too shallow for the boat and it's easier to—"

Before Izzy could finish, Sitara had swung her legs over the side and there was a splash. She stood in the water, her pants soaked from her thighs down. Now her hijab had completely fallen down around her neck.

Izzy wasn't sure what to say, but before she could think of something, Flotsam leapt out and swam to shore. He scurried onto the beach and shook, sending water drops flying. Sitara laughed.

"Well, if everyone else is getting out . . ." Izzy jumped in too. "The water is so warm today."

Sitara dropped the weight into the water. "About six and a half knots," she shouted.

"That's about thirty-nine inches or three and a

quarter feet." Izzy recorded the measurement. They kept going until the area was finished. "I was able to do that twice as fast with your help," Izzy said.

When the wind began to kick up, Izzy added, "I guess we better head back." They climbed into the boat and she pulled up the anchor, securing it under her seat.

"How did you learn how to do this?" Sitara asked.

Izzy shrugged. "Marie Tharp. She was the woman I told you about who mapped the ocean floor."

"She taught you?" Sitara asked.

"No." Izzy laughed. "I read a book about her life. Before she mapped the ocean floor, no one knew what it looked like."

"Did Marie Tharp take soundings the same way we did?"

"No. Actually, at the beginning of her career the men who ran the research vessels wouldn't let her go on the boats because they said women were bad luck."

"That's really dumb," Sitara said.

"I know, right?"

"How did she make her maps, then?"

"She used the soundings data that the men who got to go on the research vessels collected—but they used

194

sonar. They'd send a soundwave to the ocean floor and they'd measure how long it took to come back. They gave her the data and she charted it. She was really smart."

"You are really smart, Izzy," Sitara said. "Thank you for teaching me how to take soundings."

Izzy blushed. She had never had a friend tell her she was smart before. "Thanks," she said. "It's really no big deal." She started the engine and began to head back to the marina.

As they neared the breachway, the water inside the channel rose and fell. Waves slammed against its boulders, erupting in a frothy spray.

"Why is that water so angry?" Sitara asked.

Izzy laughed. "I think it looks angry too. It's the breachway. It's where the pond meets the ocean."

"It looks like a pot of boiling water," Sitara said. "What makes it . . . how do you say?" She spun her hands around in a commotion.

"Churn? When it turns low tide in the pond, the water empties into the Atlantic. But at the same time, the Atlantic's waves are heading into the pond—and it all meets inside this narrow channel. Plus, when there's an easterly wind, like today, it makes it even rougher."

"Can we go there?" Sitara asked.

Izzy shook her head. "I'm scared to go near the breachway. I'm worried it will pull us into the Atlantic."

"Did your father say that you can't go there?"

"No, he says I can handle it if I stay in front of the current."

Sitara sat up. "Then we must go."

"Um . . . why?"

"Because after you do it, you won't be scared anymore."

"Easy for you to say. I'll stay in the pond, thank you very much."

"The pond *is* nice." Sitara jutted out her chin. "But if we never go beyond it, we will never know what it's like out there," she said, pointing at the Atlantic.

Izzy peered through the narrow channel, out into the rolling gray waves. Then she looked back at Sitara.

Sitara threw her hands in the air. "How are you going to map the ocean if you won't go in it?"

"Marie made amazing maps without being on the ocean."

Sitara gave her a sideways glance. "And was that her choice?"

"No," she said. "The men wouldn't let her."

"That's another reason we must go. We must do it for Marie Tharp."

Izzy stared hard at the Atlantic. She bit the inside of her cheek.

"Don't you want to stop being afraid?" Sitara asked.

"Of course I do." She thought back to bodysurfing in the waves. The ocean had been her friend back then.

Sitara shrugged. "It's your choice, Izzy."

Izzy stared hard at Sitara. She looked different with her hijab off and her long black hair stuck to her face like wet strings. But her large, brown, unblinking eyes seemed to take on a mischievous glint.

An image of Sitara on that first day when she jumped into the skiff flashed across her brain. *Go!* she had screamed. She had seen something in Sitara then—something Izzy missed. Sitara was fearless.

"I know you can do it, Izzy," she said.

Izzy fixed her gaze on the Atlantic. Then she nodded. "You're right," she said. "Let's go."

Chapter 13

Sitara squealed with excitement as Izzy gripped the tiller and navigated the skiff into the breachway. The noise of churning water grew louder as the sound echoed back and forth against the boulders lining the narrow channel.

What have I gotten myself into? Izzy wondered. The seawater cauldron rocked the little boat. The steep boulders on either side of them seemed to stare down with grim faces.

Out and back, she thought. *No big deal.*

Flotsam, perched on the bow, gave a shrill bark, as

if to say, *Danger! Danger!* The fur on the back of his neck stood on end.

Izzy held tight, fighting to stay straight as the current pulled the skiff to the right and then to the left.

A wave crashed against the hull, drenching the girls. Sitara screamed, but held on to her seat with white knuckles. Flotsam jumped down from the bow, scrambling back and forth as if to tell Izzy, *We don't belong here!*

Stay in front of the current. Izzy could hear her father's voice in her head. *If you're faster than it, then you're in control. If you're slower—then it's in control of you.*

Right then the boat broke through. A rugged blanket of gray waves stretched in every direction. They were in the wide-open Atlantic, where the curling waves lifted the skiff right out of the water.

Izzy's head spun in every direction as the air left her lungs. Her skin tingled beneath the saltwater spray.

Sitara turned, and Izzy expected to see a look of terror, but instead, her eyes glowed with excitement.

"You did it!" she screamed over the wind and waves.

And as nervous as Izzy was, she couldn't help but smile back. *I did do it! We're in the Atlantic.*

She pumped her fist in the air. "Woo-hooo!" she screamed at the top of her lungs.

The skiff rose and fell, and the spray soaked Izzy. She quickly grabbed the tiller again so that she could steer.

Sitara stretched her arms out on either side of her like wings. "We are magical mërghëy," she shouted. "We can do anything!"

"Wooooo-hooooo!" Izzy yelled again as a wave hit the bow, spraying water down the length of the skiff. The boat was spinning. She knew if a wave broadsided them, they would capsize.

She grabbed the tiller and steered the tiny boat awkwardly around. Up and down it went in the waves. On an up motion, the small boat's propeller was lifted out of the water enough to make it whine in the empty air. Splash, the boat plunged down again with a crash.

The ocean was everywhere—it roared in her ears and drenched her hair. It seeped into her skin and filled her lungs. She felt as though she was seven years old and body surfing all over again. She was part of the ocean and it was part of her.

But somehow its deafening roar wasn't scary anymore. Instead, the energy of the waves had entered her bloodstream, coursing through her veins like a shooting star.

Sitara is right, she thought. *We are magical mërghëy!*

Flotsam barked, tucking himself under the bow.

Sitara leaned forward on the bench. Her hands gripped her seat, but her chin pointed up as if she didn't want to miss one second.

Up the boat went, with its whining engine. Down it slapped. They made slow progress back to the breachway as waves crashed against the hull.

Up and down and up and down again, until finally they were back within the narrow channel. Izzy fought to keep the rudder straight, against the breachway's rapid current.

And then, as if someone flipped a switch, the roar of the ocean went quiet as the tiny skiff coasted into the pond.

Izzy cut the engine and turned toward Sitara. Her hair stuck to her face and ocean water dripped from her nose. Her hijab, still loose around her neck, was soaked, as were all of her clothes. Sitara began to laugh and Izzy couldn't help but join in.

Soon the sound of their laughter echoed across the pond.

"Thank you, Izzy," Sitara said. "That was the best thing I've ever done."

"Yeah." Izzy grinned. "It was."

"I wish we could do that every day."

"If you want, I can teach you how to drive the boat."

"Really?" Sitara beamed. She put a hand up to her head. "Oh no. Mor and Baba can't see me like this. They'll never let me go with you again."

Izzy restarted the engine. "Don't worry," she said. "I know what to do."

When they returned to the dock, Izzy ran up to the house to make sure the coast was clear. Fortunately, her dad and Dr. Haidary were busy in the workshop.

She scrambled back for Sitara. "Come on!" she said. They darted through the shop and up the stairs, leaving a trail of wet footprints behind them. "Let's go to my room."

When they stumbled into the second-floor kitchen, Starenka was at the table rolling dough.

"Ack!" she said when she saw the girls.

Izzy and Sitara froze. Water puddled at their feet.

Starenka shook her head. "I see nothing!" she said as she continued to roll her dough.

The girls laughed as they tumbled into Izzy's room.

Izzy grabbed pants and a T-shirt from her bureau and handed them to Sitara. "Put these on while I dry your stuff," she said as she stepped out of the room. "When you're ready, hand me your wet clothes."

Soon Sitara's hand reached out with her dripping clothes. Izzy put them in the dryer, then went into the bathroom to change.

When she came back to her room, Sitara was sitting on the bed wearing Izzy's long-sleeved, hot-pink JIM'S DOCK T-shirt and blue jeans. "Thank you for lending me these clothes," she said.

"You can borrow them anytime."

Sitara pulled her hair back.

"I have one of my mom's scarves," Izzy said. "Until yours dries, you can make it into a hijab if you want." Izzy rummaged through her drawers and pulled out a soft pink gauze scarf. She handed it to Sitara.

"Do you want me to show you how to wear hijab?" Sitara asked.

"Um . . . okay," Izzy said.

Sitara took the scarf and folded it in half. She placed the crease across Izzy's forehead, then pulled the sides tight around her face. Finally, she tucked the ends across her chin.

"Do you have a pin?"

Holding the fabric in place so that it wouldn't come undone, Izzy rummaged through a drawer until she found one. She handed it to Sitara, who used it to fasten the scarf in place.

Izzy held up a mirror. "Wow. I look so different." The hijab gave her a warm, secure feeling.

"You look khaista," Sitara said. "It means beautiful in Pashto."

Izzy blushed, still looking at her reflection.

Sitara glanced around the room. "Our bedrooms are the same, but yours is better." She stepped in front of the World Ocean Floor Panorama. "What is this?"

"Remember I was telling you about Marie Tharp? That's a copy of the map of the ocean floor that she drew."

"This is what it looks like under the ocean?"

"Yeah, isn't it cool?"

"This is amazing. It's so detailed. These look like mountains, under the sea."

"Yeah, there are mountains, valleys, even volcanoes. See this?" Izzy pointed to a long chain of mountains that encircled the earth like a backbone. "When Marie discovered this ridge, she finally proved that the continents do move—just like Ms. Sardo was talking about last time in class."

Sitara walked over to the growing map of Oceanside Pond. "You drew all of this?"

"Yup. Every time I finish a section, I add it to where it belongs on the pond. What we measured today will go here." She tapped a cove located on the bottom center of the map.

Sitara guided her finger through the breachway to the Atlantic and back. "This is where we went."

Izzy thought about how terrified she was as they fought their way through the breachway, and how Sitara hadn't flinched. She remembered how Sitara had skipped across the roof on that night they had traveled to "Narnia," and how she had done the news alone, when Izzy was too nervous to join her.

"You're not scared of anything," Izzy said.

"Me?" Sitara laughed. "I'm scared of everything. Every day I'm scared to talk in class because I might say something very stupid. I'm scared that I will do something to bring shame to my parents. I'm scared I will never get to be a lawyer like Maria Bashir."

"You don't act scared. You act brave."

"It's the same thing." Sitara sat back on the bed.

"No, it's not."

"Yes, it is." Sitara said. "Being brave is when you are very scared of something—but you do it anyway. Like Maria Bashir."

"What did Maria Bashir do that was so brave?"

"She's a lawyer in Afghanistan. When the Taliban wouldn't let her help women in courts anymore, she started a secret school for girls in her house. The Taliban threatened to kill her and her family. She and her children had to hide. But still, Maria Bashir continued her work. I know she must have been scared, but she kept doing it anyway. That's brave."

"The Taliban told her they would kill her because she was helping girls?" Izzy sat next to her.

"Yes."

"You must be glad you're not in Afghanistan anymore."

Sitara looked out the window. "I miss my home very much. I miss my family and friends. I'm happy to be here, but if I could choose—I would choose home."

Again, Izzy felt a stab of guilt. She wished she hadn't heard their fathers talking earlier.

"What was it like . . . I mean, it must have been so different there. What was your school like?"

"Well, first, there were only girls in my school. We worked very hard. Every day I was doing memorization and giving presentations. We also attended classes six days a week—every day except Friday."

Izzy raised her eyebrows. "Six days!"

"I liked my school in Kabul— but we didn't have anything like the television news. It's my favorite class."

"It's okay, I guess." Izzy looked at her hands. "Except the talking part."

Sitara laughed. "That's the best part of all. It's a chance . . . I don't know . . . to have people listen to what you have to say. Most people don't get that chance, you know what I mean?"

"No."

Sitara leaned back and looked at the ceiling. "In

Afghanistan, there's much chaos. Much noise. No one listens—especially to girls." She took a breath. "You know when I spoke about hijab?"

"Yes."

"I wanted to do that because I see people stare and point. They have made up in their minds about what they think hijab means or what it means to be Muslim—but most people are wrong. They're looking on the outside of me and making their opinions. They don't know what I am like on the inside. Some people don't want to bother to learn. But the news—it gives me the opportunity to speak about real facts instead of pretend guesses—and the whole school is listening!"

"Wow," Izzy said. "When you say it like that, I guess it *is* pretty powerful."

"Yes," Sitara said. "Words can have good power and bad power."

Izzy thought back to the ugly words scratched into the bathroom stalls. Once she'd seen them, she couldn't unsee them. And even though they weren't about her, they still hurt.

"I still don't really understand why you wear the hijab. I mean . . . I know what you said on the news at school, but if you took it off, maybe kids like Apollo would leave you alone."

"It's my choice to wear hijab because of my religion. But what's most important for me is that hijab is a reminder of who I am. It helps me hold on to my home." Sitara shook her head. "I won't let anyone make me feel ashamed of something they don't understand."

Ever since Izzy had met Sitara, she had looked at Sitara's hijab as an accessory—like a necklace or a hair ribbon. But it wasn't those things at all. Sitara's hijab was sacred. It was also a part of who she was.

"Do you think the dryer is finished now?" Sitara asked.

"Let me check." Izzy came back with Sitara's hijab, clean and dry. She watched her expertly wrap it around her head.

Sitara stared down at the JIM'S DOCK T-shirt. "Is it okay if I keep wearing these today?"

"Sure." Izzy grinned as she touched her hand to her new hijab. "Keep them as long as you like."

Chapter 14

On Monday afternoon, Izzy made her way to science. As she took her seat, she glanced back to see Zelda talking to Apollo, who was doing some stupid thing where he was trying to make his fidget spinner twirl on his nose. It kept falling off and Zelda was laughing as if it was the funniest thing she'd ever seen.

"Hi, Izzy, did you finish your homework?" Sitara asked as she sat next to her.

Before Izzy had a chance to answer, Ms. Sardo stood at the front of the room. "Okay, friends, let's get started," she said. The image of Pangaea materialized on the board. "We are going to continue with our study of plate tectonics."

She pushed a button, and the big blob of land in the center of the screen broke apart like last time, morphing into the present-day globe. "As we discussed, scientists were quick to dismiss Alfred Wegener's theories that the continents actually moved. Some even mocked him. Wegener's problem was that he didn't have the scientific evidence necessary to back up his theory."

She clicked the remote and an image of Marie Tharp's World Ocean Floor Panorama materialized.

"Izzy!" Sitara whispered. "It's the same map as in your room."

"Today we will discuss how a scientist named Marie Tharp completely changed how scientists understood the oceans," Ms. Sardo continued. "Like Wegener, she asked a question no one had asked before—what does the ocean floor really look like?

"At the time, scientists assumed it was flat. But based on maps that Tharp had drawn from actual sounding records, she knew they were wrong."

Sitara's hand shot up.

"Yes, Sitara?" Ms. Sardo said.

"Izzy and I did this on Sunday. Except, instead of sonar, Izzy uses a string attached to a weight. Izzy is mapping Oceanside Pond with this string and weight."

Ms. Sardo turned to Izzy. "Really? That's amazing. Do you have the maps with you?"

Izzy felt her ears get hot, but she couldn't help but smile and nod.

"That's awesome! At the end of class, would you mind displaying them on the front table for everyone to see?"

Izzy nodded.

"It's a lot of work," Sitara said. "But Izzy is really good at it."

Izzy bit the inside of her cheek. She glanced over to see if Zelda was listening and whether she'd noticed how excited Ms. Sardo got about her maps. *Maybe Zelda will want to talk about the time we went measuring together?* Izzy thought. But when Izzy tried to make eye contact with her, Zelda crossed her arms and looked away.

Ms. Sardo continued. "Over the thirty years since Wegener's theory had been proposed, scientists had come up with a new theory called plate tectonics.

212

They thought plates were being forced apart by deep-sea earthquakes and volcanoes. Still," she said, "it was only a theory—until Marie Tharp."

Directing the remote at the screen, Ms. Sardo highlighted the deep crack running between the mountain peaks of the Mid-Atlantic Ridge. "Even with the sounding data collected by research vessels and meticulously plotted by Marie Tharp, scientists continued to dismiss what her maps clearly showed.

"For so long, they had believed that the ocean floor was flat; they didn't want to consider anything else. But Marie Tharp didn't waver. She knew how carefully she had charted the data. She knew she was right.

"Finally, a scientist named Jacques Cousteau was so confident that Marie Tharp's maps were wrong, he brought a camera to the bottom of the ocean so he could prove it. But Cousteau's footage proved the opposite. It revealed images of the Mid-Atlantic Ridge that Tharp had mapped.

"Now, because I want you to learn to ask good questions like Alfred Wegener and Marie Tharp, I'm going to pass out a piece of paper. I want each of you to draw what you think the world will look like a thousand years from now.

"Remember, the continents have not stopped moving. I want to see where you predict things will end up, and I want to hear your theory for why it will happen that way."

Apollo stood. On his way to the pencil sharpener, he pretended to lose his balance. Kids laughed.

"Is there a problem, Apollo?"

"North America must be moving again, Ms. Sardo," he said.

"Go sit down, Apollo," she said.

When everyone had started drawing, Ms. Sardo approached Izzy. "Thanks for agreeing to share your maps, Izzy. If you don't mind spreading them out on the front desk, everyone can take turns looking at them."

Izzy beamed, removing the maps from her patchwork bag. Sitara joined her, looking just as excited about watching Izzy share her maps as Izzy was herself.

Again, Izzy glanced back, trying to make eye contact with Zelda. But she was so busy talking to Apollo, she didn't seem to notice.

When the bell rang, Zelda gathered her things and hustled out. Izzy quickly tucked away her maps and darted after her. But when she stepped into the hallway, Zelda was already gone.

The next day, as Izzy and Sitara made their way to the bus stop, Sitara seemed quieter than usual.

"Do you want to take soundings around the oyster farm after school?" Izzy asked.

Sitara shrugged. "Maybe."

"Are you okay?" Izzy asked.

Sitara nodded but she looked away.

Izzy fought with her locker again that morning. After the third try she threw her hands in the air. "This thing is broken," she said. Sitara leaned over. With three quick turns, the locker popped open.

"How do you do that?" Izzy said.

But Sitara didn't answer. Instead she stared blankly inside her own locker.

"Sitara?" Izzy said. "What's wrong?"

Sitara shut her locker. Tears poked out from the corners of her eyes. "I'm going to the ladies' room," she said, and walked away.

Izzy watched her go, wondering if she should follow.

"Hey!" It was Piper.

"Hi," Izzy said.

"What are you doing? The first bell already rang; come on."

Izzy followed her into tech ed.

As they entered, Roger and Nathaniel were sitting at the computer. Izzy panicked. She'd been doing script every day since she'd freaked out about being assigned anchor. She scrambled to the assignment board, scanning it for her name. SOUND: MANCINI/HAIDARY; COPY: RICHARDS/JOHNSON; ANCHOR: AKINS/GRENIER; GRAPHICS: ALLEN. Izzy exhaled as she made her way to the control room.

When she got there, Taylor was showing Zelda how to work the sound board with its rows of complicated buttons. They were both wearing headphones. Izzy stood, waiting for them to notice her.

"Um. Sitara and I are on sound," she finally said.

Zelda held a finger up as if to say *one minute*.

"I was showing Zelda how everything works," Tay-

216

lor said. "Now she can show you." Taylor handed Izzy her headphones and headed over to the graphics computer.

Izzy took her seat.

Zelda continued to adjust dials.

"So, what am I supposed to do?" Izzy said. She could hear music coming from Zelda's headphones.

Zelda didn't answer.

Maybe she can't hear me, Izzy thought. She tapped her on the shoulder, but Zelda continued to adjust the dials, as if Izzy weren't even there.

Izzy swallowed hard.

Piper had taken her seat at the anchor desk. Mr. Cantor was reading over Nathaniel's and Roger's shoulders. Sitara was staring blankly at the assignment board. With her head down, she made her way to the control room. Soon she stood behind Zelda.

Zelda didn't budge.

"Excuse me," Sitara finally said. Her voice came out in a whisper. Her eyes looked puffy and red.

Zelda removed her headphones and put them down. "You're not going to be able to hear with that thing on your head. You should take it off."

Sitara ignored her as she took her seat. She put the headphones on over her hijab.

"We haven't done this before. Can you tell us what we need to do?" Izzy asked.

Zelda paused in the doorway, and Izzy's heart leapt for a moment. Maybe all this silent treatment stuff was in her head after all.

"By the way," Zelda said.

Izzy waited.

"We aren't doing those stupid sea star facts anymore." Zelda walked away.

Izzy blinked hard at the rows of buttons and dials in front of her. Her cheeks felt hot, as if actually stung by Zelda's words.

"I don't know what to do," she said to no one in particular.

Taylor spun around in her chair. "Zelda already picked the music and has it all set up, so it will be easy today." She walked over. "The biggest job is to moderate the sound. What you hear on the earphones is what it will sound like on the recording." She pointed to the bottom row of dials. "These control volume, bass, and treble. You can adjust them if the anchors' voices are coming through too soft or loud. And you need to signal Mr. Cantor if the sound cuts out or anything else goes wrong." She pointed to a switch. "At the end, hold this button down while flicking this switch, and the closing song will play." Taylor returned to the graphics computer. "I'll be right here. Signal me if you have a question."

Izzy looked at all the buttons. The angry-ocean sound was starting in her ears. *Not now*, she told it. She leaned closer to Sitara. "Did you get all that?" she asked.

Sitara stared into space.

"What is going on with you today?"

But Sitara only gave Izzy a blank look as if she didn't understand what she was asking.

"Five, four . . ." Mr. Cantor stood in the middle of the studio, wearing a rainbow bow tie. He lowered his fingers. *Three, two, one.*

"Good morning. Today is Tuesday, September eleventh, and this is your Shoreline Regional Middle School news," Piper said.

"Today is National Day of Service and Remembrance," Zelda added.

"Lunch is taco/nacho bar," Piper said.

"On this day in history, in 2001," Zelda said, "a series of four coordinated suicide attacks were carried out by the terrorist group al-Qaeda, led by Osama bin Laden. The terrorists used commercial airplanes to crash into the World Trade Center towers."

Piper continued, "The terrorists also crashed a plane into the Pentagon building, but passengers aboard a fourth plane fought back, causing that plane to crash into a field in Pennsylvania. Almost three thousand Americans lost their lives. These attacks led to the War Against Terror and the War in Afghanistan."

Although Izzy wasn't born yet when 9/11 happened, she had heard her father and mother talk about it. She knew that it was the reason her dad's National Guard troop deployed to Afghanistan. Izzy looked around. Everyone was glued to the broadcast. The studio was always quiet while recording, but during that report, the quiet felt different.

"This is Piper Grenier."

"And Zelda Akins."

There was an awkward pause.

Zelda squinted at Izzy through the window.

Piper mouthed the word, *Music?*

Oh no! Izzy thought. She looked at the rows of buttons, trying to remember which one to flick and which one to switch. She frantically shook her head, *NO*.

Piper turned back toward the camera. "See you tomorrow for more Shoreline Regional Middle School news."

Mr. Cantor nodded. "Cut!"

Izzy removed her headphones and ran into the studio, Sitara behind her.

Zelda yanked her mic off. "What happened?" she yelled. "Sound should have had the music ready."

"I liked it," Roger said. "It was like we had a moment of silence."

"I agree," Mr. Cantor said. "I think it was a good choice given the subject matter." He nodded. "Silence can be more powerful than words." He turned toward Izzy and Sitara. "Next time, please loop us all in on your plan, okay?"

Izzy and Sitara looked at each other.

"Let's see how graphics are coming along." Mr. Cantor made his way into the control room. Piper and Zelda started to follow.

As they passed, Zelda paused to glare at Sitara.

"Did you really skip the music for effect or were you trying to ruin today's news?"

"It was a mistake!" Izzy said. "No one really showed us what we were supposed to do."

Zelda narrowed her eyes at Sitara. "Maybe you didn't like what we were saying about your friends."

Sitara's puffy eyes turned glassy all over again.

Piper tugged at Zelda. "Come on," she said. "It was a mistake."

Zelda wouldn't budge. "You know," she said to Sitara, "you look like Osama bin Laden with that thing wrapped around your head. I can't believe you would wear that today."

Izzy opened her mouth as if to say something; then she turned to Sitara, whose cheeks had turned bright pink.

"Forget it, Zelda," Piper said. This time when Piper pulled, Zelda followed her into the control room.

"They think it was my fault," Sitara whispered.

Izzy shook her head. "It was me. I—I just forgot. It was a mistake."

"But they didn't blame you, Izzy. They blamed me."

Sitara turned to face Izzy, tears streaking her face. "And you didn't say anything."

"I—I didn't know what to say."

Sitara turned on her heel and walked toward the door.

"Where are you going?" Izzy took a step to follow her. Then stopped.

Sitara disappeared into the hallway.

Izzy looked into the control room. Everyone was busy with graphics. Izzy began to head in there, then froze. She didn't want to face Zelda and her accusations.

She crossed her arms and stared into the empty hall, waiting for Sitara to come back.

But Sitara never did.

Fourth Grade

Surf camp was Zelda's idea. It was the summer after third grade and most of the kids doing it were summer renters and teenagers.

I remember fighting my way into my wet suit and booties. They were still wet and sandy from whoever used them last, and I had to tug hard to get them on. The sand made my skin itch.

Zelda was the first one ready. "This is so cool," she kept saying.

We had to walk from South Kingstown Town Beach, past the Ocean Mist, all the way to Deep Hole. Piper stayed at the back of the crowd with me, while Zelda walked up front with the instructors. She spent the whole time talking to Sean, who was old enough to drive, and wore purple zinc oxide on his nose.

Even though it was hot, and my booties were giving me blisters, I didn't want the walk to end because I knew that when it did, I'd have to surf.

The beach at Deep Hole was rough and rocky. I already missed Brogee's. We laid our boards in the sand and practiced popping up to catch a wave.

"Good job, Izzy." Sean gave me a thumbs-up.

"How's this, Sean?" Zelda asked, springing into a surfer's stance.

"You're a natural!"

Everyone grabbed their boards and headed into the water. Piper and I followed Zelda as she paddled out.

"Come on!" she said. "There's bigger waves over there."

Piper shrugged, but followed.

I didn't want to be left behind so I paddled too. When I reached Zelda and Piper, I turned my surfboard around. The beach was so far away that our instructors looked like tiny dots.

The waves took me up and down. Up and down.

"Woo-hoo!" Zelda was the first one up, riding a wave in. Soon Piper caught one too.

I lay on my surfboard, unable to loosen my grip.

As the two of them rode toward shore, the sound of the ocean grew loud in my ears. The waves were pulling

me in the wrong direction. The beach was moving far-
ther and farther away.

Suddenly, I heard a whistle. Sean and the other in-
structors were waving their arms, telling me to come in.

But the ocean sound only got angrier—it filled my
ears and my head. I was too scared to let go of my
board to paddle.

Then Sean was in the water, coming toward me. But
as hard as he paddled and as swiftly as he moved, the
ocean brought me farther in the other direction.

I kept thinking about the movie Soul Surfer, *when*
Bethany Hamilton's arm got bit off by a shark. I began
to cry.

Another instructor, Grace, was in the water, follow-
ing Sean.

They were both shouting something, but I couldn't
hear them over the sound of the ocean's angry roar.

Then Sean was next to me, his blond curls slicked
back by the ocean. "Where ya goin'?" he asked.

I couldn't answer.

"Hold on," he said as he towed me back to shore.
Soon, Grace reached us and helped pull. When we

were in the shallow, rocky water she said, "Okay, you can stand now."

When I tried, my legs wouldn't work. Sean helped me up as Grace grabbed my board.

Piper and Zelda ran into the water. I could tell Piper had been crying too. "Are you okay?" she asked.

I coughed and wiped my nose. When we were on the beach, Piper wrapped her towel around my shoulders.

"You're okay, Izzy," she kept saying.

"Why didn't you paddle?" Zelda said.

Chapter 15

Izzy didn't find Sitara again until math.

"Where did you go?" Izzy asked her.

"I met with my guidance counselor. I'm quitting the news."

"What? But you love the news."

Sitara looked away.

"You said it's a way to talk to a lot of people—to make them listen."

"I have nothing left to say."

Ever since middle school had begun, Izzy had

wanted to quit the news. But hearing Sitara say that seemed so wrong.

Sitara pressed her lips together, as if to keep from crying.

Izzy didn't understand what was happening—to the Sea Stars—to Sitara. The only thing she did know was that no matter how hard she tried to keep her head above water, the ocean just kept rising. *If I could just talk to Zelda and Piper alone*, Izzy thought, *I could explain that it's all been a misunderstanding.*

At that moment, Zelda entered the room, walking past the empty seat next to Izzy to sit with Apollo. Izzy watched him pass her a note. Zelda opened it and started laughing. Then she looked directly at Izzy and smirked.

Izzy's stomach sank.

Zelda was sending her a direct message: *Even Apollo is better than you.*

After language arts, Izzy made a beeline to the cafeteria to find Zelda and Piper before Sitara got there. Not only did she need to get the Sea Stars alone, she knew she needed Piper there to make Zelda listen.

Then she'll see that forgetting to play the music was a mistake—my mistake, not Sitara's.

When Izzy stepped into the cafeteria, she immediately found Piper and Zelda, sitting next to each other at their usual table, deep in conversation. Piper smiled and waved.

Izzy took a deep breath. *We are the Sea Stars*, she reminded herself. *Best friends forever.* She walked over and stood in front of Zelda so that she'd have to face her.

"Hey," Piper said.

"We need to talk," Izzy began.

But Zelda wouldn't meet her gaze.

"Zelda," Izzy said.

Zelda seemed to be looking around her. Then, Zelda leaned in close to Piper and whispered something.

Izzy spun around to see Apollo standing behind Sitara—still wearing that stupid grin—just as he had the other day.

Sitara waved at Izzy and began walking toward her. But Apollo was faster this time. Before Sitara knew what was happening, he reached up and swiped Sitara's hijab off her head.

As Sitara's hands flew up, she dropped her lunch. A container of rice spilled across the floor.

"Noooooooo!" Izzy shouted.

But it was too late. She watched in horror as Sitara's long, silky black hair fell across her shoulders.

For a moment, it seemed as if everyone in the cafeteria inhaled at the same time, sucking in all the noise and chaos and chatter that normally consumed lunchtime.

Sitara had frozen—locked midway between a scream and a cry, finally giving up on the impossible job of covering her hair and face with her hands.

Apollo stared at the hijab in his hand and then glanced around the cafeteria as if waiting for the laughter and applause he thought he'd just earned.

"You're an idiot!" a girl yelled.

"Give it back to her!" someone else shouted.

"What's the matter with you?" another voice screamed.

"Loser! Give it back!"

Sitara ran out of the cafeteria, her face in her hands.

Izzy's mouth opened. *Sitara!* she tried to yell. But the words stuck in her throat.

Two cafeteria aides were on either side of Apollo. One took the hijab away from him. The other escorted him away.

Izzy ran out too. She didn't know where to go, but she had to find Sitara. She ran down the empty hallway. Nothing. She turned down the next hallway, and kept running.

Empty. Empty. Empty.

"Slow down!" a teacher yelled. But Izzy didn't care. She took off again down another hallway until she came to their lockers. But Sitara wasn't there either. The first bell rang.

Izzy ducked into the bathroom. "Sitara?" she called. Nothing.

Izzy stared into the mirror, but instead of seeing her own reflection, an image of Sitara seemed to materialize before her—Sitara, standing in the cafeteria without her hijab.

Izzy shut her eyes, but the image wouldn't go away, instead playing like one of those YouTube movies that they used to watch at their all-night sleepovers. Sitara—her hands flying up—trying to cover her hair, trying to cover her face. Although she hadn't spoken a word, her eyes seemed to ask a question: Why?

Izzy knew that Sitara was not asking Apollo why he had done what he did. She was not asking Zelda why she was laughing. She was asking Izzy *Why? Why are you just standing there? Why aren't you saying something? Why aren't you doing something?*

Feeling bad when someone's being treated poorly is fine and all, Izzy, but until you actually do something to change things . . . well, what's the point?

Izzy turned on the faucet and splashed water on her face.

She didn't have an answer.

Sitara wasn't in social studies or science. And she wasn't on the bus home.

When Izzy got to her stop, Dad was waiting.

"What are you doing here?" she asked him.

And even though his smile hadn't been the same since Afghanistan, right then it seemed even sadder. "Do I need a reason to walk my daughter home?"

As they made their way to the marina, Izzy hugged

her patchwork bag. "You heard what happened at school."

Her father nodded. "Are you okay?"

"Yes." She kicked a rock and it skittered across the road. "It happened to Sitara, not me."

"Hate hurts everyone."

Izzy bit her lip. "Is she home?"

Her father nodded.

"Is she okay?"

Her father shook his head.

"I didn't know what to do, Dad. It happened so fast." The tears she'd fought to hold back all afternoon began to escape, running down her face in crooked streaks.

Her father put his arm around her.

After a moment Izzy said, "Dr. and Mrs. Haidary must be really mad."

"Mostly sad. And worried."

"Is—do you know if Sitara's mad at me?"

"For what?"

Izzy shrugged.

When they got to the boatyard, her father gave her a hug. She wiped her tears on his shirt.

"Are you sure you're okay?" he asked.

Izzy nodded.

"You should go talk to her. I think it will make you both feel better."

Izzy watched him walk toward the mechanics' workshop.

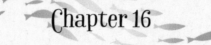

Chapter 16

Outside the Haidarys' door, Izzy took a deep breath. Then knocked.

Mrs. Haidary answered, and the scent of cardamom wafted out. Izzy's stomach rumbled, and she couldn't help but think back to the delicious melmastiyâ feast.

"Is Sitara home?" Izzy asked.

"Dënana râsha." Mrs. Haidary motioned her inside. Izzy silently followed her to Sitara's room.

Mrs. Haidary knocked on her door. "Sitara?" she said softly, and then something else in her language.

She gave Izzy a sad smile before returning to the kitchen.

Sitara's door opened. She was wearing a different hijab than the one Apollo had swiped. Izzy wondered if she'd gotten that one back from the cafeteria aide. *If it was mine*, Izzy thought, *I'd never want to wear it again.* Apollo had ruined it.

"Can I come in?" Izzy asked.

Sitara left the door open, then sat on her mattress. Books and papers were scattered across her bed. Her journal was open.

"What are you doing?" Izzy asked.

"Writing," Sitara said.

"Apollo got suspended," Izzy said.

"I know."

"So, he won't bother you at school anymore."

"It doesn't matter. I'm not going back."

"What do you mean you're not going back? You have to."

"The school called my parents and they told them what happened." Sitara's voice caught for a moment and then she continued. "My parents said that I can do my studies on my own if I want. I don't need school. I don't need anyone."

Izzy felt as though she'd been punched in the gut.

"Is that what *you* want?"

Sitara picked up her science book.

"B-but you love school. And Apollo—he got punished. It won't happen again."

Sitara shook her head. "There are many Apollos. It will happen again."

"What about the news and astronomy club? You told me—" Izzy's mouth twisted, trying to find the right words that would convince Sitara that she was making a mistake. "Maria Bashir!" she shouted. "She wouldn't let a bully make her quit. She'd keep fighting. Isn't that what you told me? Even when the Taliban threatened to kill her, she didn't give up!"

Sitara slammed her science book shut. "You don't know anything!"

Izzy fell back from the power of Sitara's voice. When she regained her own, she said, "Well, tell me, then."

"You wouldn't . . . you can't understand." A gust blew in through the opened window, rustling the papers spread across her mattress.

Izzy sat on the edge. "I can try."

Sitara stared out the window. "There are many

kinds of bullies, Izzy. Apollo was not the first and he will not be the last."

Izzy waited.

"In Afghanistan, it started with a letter—threats delivered by the Taliban in the middle of the night. It was nailed to the front door of our home in Khost." She took a deep breath, and Izzy could tell it was hard for her to talk about it.

Sitara frowned. "The first one said, *You are a traitor.* Then there were more. Notes that said, *You have helped the Americans. Now you will die* and *We will kill your wife and children.*" Tears filled Sitara's large brown eyes. "I couldn't go to school. I couldn't go to the park. I couldn't see my friends. We were like prisoners in our own home. It was no life."

Izzy didn't know what to say.

"Baba moved Mor and my brothers and me to an apartment in Kabul while he kept working for the American army. Because the Taliban had made him a target, he applied for a Special Immigrant Visa for all of us. It took a year, but when he finally got it, we were so excited." She turned to Izzy. "Your government is not granting these visas as they had in the past. We were very lucky." Her large brown eyes seemed to be searching. "But still I couldn't tell anyone we were leaving."

"Why not?"

Sitara shrugged. "It was hard to know who we could trust and who might tell the Taliban about our plans." She sighed. "So we must leave in silence. I never got to say goodbye to my friends." Tears streamed down her face. "We had to disappear as if we had never existed."

Izzy wanted to leap up and hug Sitara. But even though she sat right in front of her, she felt far away too.

"We traveled all night. I had never been on a plane. We went to Dubai, then across the ocean to New York. When I saw this city, I thought, *What is this place with its noise and flashing lights?* Mor cried the whole car ride from Kennedy Airport to New Haven. Ali threw up."

"I'm so sorry, Sitara," Izzy whispered. She wanted to say, *I didn't know . . . No one told me any of that.* But she knew that she hadn't asked either.

Sitara wiped her face with the back of her hand. "The people from the refugee organization took us to our new apartment. It was so different. The rooms were small. I was thirsty but the water tasted bad.

In Afghanistan, we only lived with people we were related to, but now strangers walked with heavy steps above us, and loud music played next to us. Mor was always nervous."

She took a deep breath. "But the people from the refugee organization were so kind—you know when you look in someone's eyes and you can tell right away if they're angry, or sad, or mean—with these people I only saw good—I knew that everything would be okay. We were finally safe."

Sitara turned away. "But we weren't. A few months later, Mor found a note in our mailbox that said, *Go back to your country, terrorists.*" She swallowed. "Baba said to ignore it, but then another came. It said, *I give you twenty-four hours to leave or I will cut your heads off.*"

Izzy bit her lip as tears sprang to her eyes.

"Mor was crying. I was crying. Baba went to the police and they kept the notes. There was a police officer who sat in his car outside our apartment building every day. Mor said we must keep all the shades down. It was always dark. There was no more school for us. I was in prison all over again."

"Is that why you left Connecticut?" Izzy asked.

Sitara nodded. "Your father called and we came here and I was so happy to go outside whenever I wanted. I was happy for this fresh air and that I could go back to school." She fixed her gaze on Izzy. "I was so happy to make my first friend in the United States."

Right then Izzy wished that was the end of Sitara's story. That she came to Seabury and made a new friend and went to school, where she could do the news and astronomy club.

"But the hate has found us again." Sitara nodded slowly. "At first I tried to pretend that the whispering and pointing was nothing. I thought if I explained who I am and why I dress differently, then everyone would understand. When we came to the United States, Mor said, 'Everyone is an immigrant in the US. It is okay to look different there.'" Sitara shook her head. "But Mor was wrong."

Sitara stood up and opened a drawer in her nightstand. She removed something and held it up. Her shoulders slumped. "All I took from Afghanistan was my Qur'ân, my journal, my clothes, and this stone. It is from outside our home in Khost." She shrugged. "I know it seems silly to carry a rock all the way from Afghanistan, but it was a way for me to hold on to a piece of my country—a piece of my home."

Izzy reflexively shoved her hand inside her pocket, feeling for the house key she always carried. "I don't think it's silly at all," she said.

"I didn't even tell my parents that I took it." Sitara smiled briefly, then her smile vanished. She closed her fingers, gripping the stone in a tight fist. "I have kept it as a promise that I won't forget Afghanistan. I have kept it as a dream that someday I will find my home again." Sitara looked hard at Izzy. "But last night, I learned from my parents that the Taliban came to our home in Khost. They went through the rooms, taking whatever they could steal and sell. They broke our furniture and destroyed our photographs. When there was nothing left, they burned our house to the ground." Sitara slumped back onto the mattress. "It's gone. Everything," Sitara said. "Now I have no home here and no home in Afghanistan."

Izzy felt as if she'd been kicked in the stomach. Sitara had finally learned what Izzy had already overheard her father and Dr. Haidary discussing—that there

243

would be no going home again for the Haidarys. Ever. That was why she had been sad before school had even begun that day—before Zelda had accused her of something she hadn't done and called her a hateful name. Before Apollo had violated her with his ignorance.

"Sitara, I—" Izzy began, but the words cut against her throat.

"It doesn't matter where we go, Izzy. There will always be more hate." Sitara walked over to her wastebasket and let the stone fall into it. Then she sat back down on the mattress and hugged her knees. "I'm done with dreams."

"Sitara, you need to . . . I don't know . . . you can't just let them . . ." Her words drifted. "If you quit, then they win."

Sitara's gaze remained fixed on the books and papers scattered across the mattress.

"But—it's not fair," Izzy said. "You need to stand up to them. You need to say something."

Sitara picked up her science book. "I did say something. Remember when I spoke about the hijab on the news?" She started to read. "It didn't matter."

But it did matter, Izzy wanted to say.

"I know that Apollo was alone when he pulled my hijab off, Izzy. But he wasn't alone."

Izzy wanted to pretend that she didn't know what Sitara was talking about. But deep inside, she did.

Sitara started reading her science book again.

"I guess . . . I better go." Izzy backed toward the door, but before she left, she glanced at Sitara's closet door.

Our portal to Narnia.

She thought back to that night when they sat on the roof, gazing at the stars. She had already met Sitara then—but Narnia was where she first got to *know* her. Izzy missed that Sitara—the one who was ready to take on the world.

She stepped out of the bedroom, closing the door quietly behind her. In the kitchen, Mrs. Haidary was at the stove stirring. "Izzy! Izzy!"

A large pot steamed with wonderful smells. Izzy's stomach rumbled.

Mrs. Haidary held out a bowl wrapped in tinfoil. "Mehrebani wakrëy," she said.

Izzy tried to remember what Sitara had taught her for *thank you.* "Manana," she finally said.

Mrs. Haidary gently put her hand against Izzy's

face, as Izzy's mother had done many times and spoke to Izzy in Pashto in her soft, gentle voice. Izzy didn't know the words, but she understood everything.

Mrs. Haidary lifted Izzy's chin so they were eye to eye. Izzy felt that within that gaze Mrs. Haidary was infusing her with her bravery and confidence—as if she were giving Izzy the power she had gained through every challenge she had overcome. Without a word, she was letting Izzy know that everything would be okay—they had been through worse. The Apollos of the world were no match for the Haidarys. Then she said the first English words Izzy had heard Mrs. Haidary ever say. "Daughter," she said. "Good."

Mrs. Haidary let her hand drop, and turned back to stirring and humming.

Izzy stood a moment, touching her cheek where Mrs. Haidary's hand had been. Then she went downstairs.

As she stood outside her own apartment door, Izzy could hear Starenka's baseball game. She opened the door a crack and saw her grandmother asleep in her chair. Izzy tiptoed past her to put the tinfoil-wrapped bowl on the counter, and then she went back outside.

She walked down the pier to the skiff, but the idea

of measuring the pond without Sitara made her stomach hurt. Instead she sat down, letting her toes dip in the water.

Soon, Flotsam found her and began scrambling back and forth, daring any seagull to even try to land.

The afternoon breeze carried the promise of autumn. Izzy shivered.

After a while, the setting sun began to paint the sky orange, as crickets sang their end-of-summer song. A flock of geese soared overhead, calling to each other in honks and squawks—a black V against the pumpkin sky. Izzy watched a smaller goose slow, falling farther and farther from its flock.

"Go, bird," she quietly cheered. "You can do it." Soon three other birds joined the slow bird, forming their own mini V.

"Ooo-hoo, what's my girl doing here?"

Izzy turned to see her grandmother walking toward her in bare feet. Her hair wasn't in its usual tight gray bun, instead falling down her back in loose silver strands.

"Hi, Starenka," Izzy said.

"Dobrý večer," Starenka said as she removed the

shawl she was wearing. She wrapped it around Izzy's shoulders before easing herself down. Her toes dipped into the water. "Ah, that feels good," she said as she squinted across the horizon. "God's painting a pretty picture tonight."

Izzy shrugged.

"You know," Starenka said, "my mother, she never talked much about coming to this country."

Izzy shook her head. *Not now, Starenka*, she wanted to say. *I'm really not in the mood.*

Her grandmother swirled her feet in the water as if she were a little girl. "My mother. I wish I had asked her more about what it was like leaving her country."

Izzy stared into the pond.

"But one time," Starenka continued, "when I was helping her hang laundry, she started to talk as if I wasn't standing right next to her. She told me how scared she was of the ocean."

"When did she see the ocean?" Starenka mother had never lived in Rhode Island.

"When she came to America, of course."

"Oh yeah," Izzy said. "Steerage and the mean girls with coins and baby Uncle Viktor."

Starenka put a hand to her heart. "My girl listens!"

Izzy rolled her eyes. "Of course I listen." She tried to fight back the smile tugging on her lips.

"Mama could barely leave their room on the ship," Starenka continued. "But one time, when everyone was asleep, she walked out to the deck. The ship was in the middle of the ocean by then, and the waves were rough. Mama said that the ocean seemed to go on forever—she thought that it was impossible that anything could be so big as that ocean. She began to panic, worrying that it would swallow that ship and with it her entire world." Starenka lifted a finger. "That ocean was like fear to Mama."

Izzy thought about surf camp and being pulled into the Atlantic at Deep Hole. She thought about how she felt as she gripped her surfboard—unable to let go long enough to save herself. The ocean had been so big—impossibly big. From that moment on, the ocean had been like fear for her too.

Her grandmother continued. "Mama and her family went to Pennsylvania and she married my father. But when he got sick from the coal mines, we moved to a farm town in Connecticut. A lot of other immigrants came too—people like us from Czechoslovakia and Hungary and Poland." Starenka shook her head. "But the people who had lived in that town their whole lives . . . they didn't like immigrants buying those farms. They didn't want us there."

"Why not?" Izzy asked.

Starenka shrugged. "We weren't like them. Our clothes, the way we talked, even our religion was different. Those folks weren't used to different." She continued, "They didn't like change. They didn't like us."

Izzy stared hard at her grandmother's profile. The way she held her chin high, and her papery skin, old and wrinkled. Her long silver hair floated in the breeze. Starenka was tiny, but she was like steel too.

"We had a milk house," Starenka continued. "It was where we stored our dairy milk before we sold it. One night, as Mama and I were closing up the barns, four men showed up. My father was not home and I could tell Mama was scared."

"Who were the men?"

"I didn't know their names, but I recognized them from town. They told Mama we were selling too much milk. They told Mama to stop.

"Mama tried to tell them we couldn't stop. Selling our milk to the cooperative was our only money." Starenka shook her head. "But Mama's English wasn't very good. The men laughed at her."

"What did she do?"

"She pulled me inside the house and locked the door."

"Did the men go away?"

"No, Isabella. They set our milk house on fire."

Izzy gasped. "Why?"

Starenka shrugged. "Maybe it was because they were jealous of how hard my parents worked. Or maybe it was because they didn't like how we were different. Maybe it was because they were bad men."

"What did you do?"

"I remember standing inside the front door of our house and stretching myself as tall as I could on my tippy toes to see out the window. I watched that fire grow." Starenka stared at the orange sunset as if the old milk house was burning right in front of her. "The men were laughing—as if destroying our property was a joke. But that milk was more than property. It was food on our table. I began to cry."

Izzy bit her lip. Her whole life, she had never seen her grandmother cry even once. Not when Izzy's grandfather died. Not when Dad left for Afghanistan. Not even when he came home.

"My mother asked me, 'Why are you crying, Iren? It's only milk. Our cows will give us more.'

"'I'm scared, Mama,' I said.

"'Bah!' Mama said. 'They are the ones who are scared.'

"'How are they scared?' I asked. 'They are the ones with the fire.'

"Mama shook her head. 'They think the fire makes them big,' she said. 'They think the fire makes them brave. So we have to be bigger. We have to be braver.'"

Starenka continued, "Right then, Mama set her jaw. I thought she was going to run out of the house and chase away those bad men—but instead she shouted, 'I didn't let the Atlantic Ocean stop me, and I won't let *you*!'"

"Did it make the men stop?"

"No, but it made them leave."

"What happened next?"

"We went outside to look at the damage. The shed was gone. All of the milk cans had melted. Pools of milk were stained black with ash. I cried even harder. But Mama looked at me and said, 'Stop, Iren.'

"'I can't, Mama,' I said. 'I'm scared.'

"'Don't be scared, Iren,' Mama said. 'Those men are to you like the Atlantic Ocean was to me. They can only scare you if you let them.'

"Then she turned to me. 'You have to decide, Iren— will your fear be bigger than your courage, or will your courage be bigger than your fear?'"

"Your mother was brave." Izzy bit her lip.

Starenka nodded. "She was." Then she turned to me. "And so are you, Isabella."

"Dad told you about what happened at school today, didn't he?"

"Ack," Starenka said. "Cowards—same as those men with the fire."

Izzy stared at her feet, large and distorted beneath the pond's surface.

"So now, granddaughter, I'm going to ask you the same question that my mama asked me. Is your fear bigger than your courage, or is your courage bigger than your fear?"

Izzy looked into Starenka's watery blue eyes. She

wanted to say, *Yes! Yes! My courage is as big as the entire Atlantic!* Instead she turned away, continuing to stare into the still pond.

As the orange sky faded to black, Izzy let her grandmother's words seep into her skin—thick and cool as the night air.

Starenka hoisted herself up with a grunt.

"You're leaving?" Izzy asked. Warmed by Starenka's shawl, her stories, and the setting sun, Izzy felt a wave of comfort begin to wash over her. She didn't want it to end.

"The game's on," Starenka said as she made her way toward the shop. "Tony Macaroni's gonna owe me money!" Her bare feet left a trail of wet footprints like bread crumbs behind her.

"Wait!" Izzy scrambled to her feet. "You didn't tell me what I'm supposed to do. How am I supposed to be brave?"

Without pausing, Starenka said, "You need to speak up, Isabella Rose."

"But what if no one listens?"

"Ack," she said. "Talk louder."

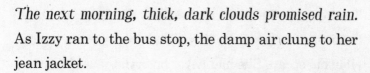

Chapter 17

The next morning, thick, dark clouds promised rain. As Izzy ran to the bus stop, the damp air clung to her jean jacket.

She sat alone as the bus wound its way through the neighborhood. When they stopped on the corner of Rosewood and Moonstone, she used her fist to wipe away a space on the fogged-up window. The cottage appeared as if it were hiding inside a cloud.

Twenty minutes later, the bus pulled into Shoreline Regional Middle—just like every morning, but completely different too.

At lunchtime, Izzy looked for Zelda and Piper. As she took a seat at their usual table, she thought about how she didn't have to worry about Sitara making things awkward anymore. *Isn't that what you had wanted all along?* Izzy asked herself. *The Sea Stars together again—just like it's always been.* Best friends forever.

But each time someone entered the cafeteria, she looked up hoping to see Sitara. When it wasn't, she had to remind herself that Sitara didn't go to school there anymore.

Rain pelted the cafeteria's long, wide windows. Thunder rumbled in the distance. She glanced about furtively, feeling like a tiny skiff bobbing in an impossibly big ocean. She had never been in the middle of so many people and still felt so alone.

She hunched her shoulders, making herself small. Noise seemed to push at her from all sides—kids shouting, trays slamming, fists pounding.

That's when she spotted Zelda and Piper sitting with Taylor's group. Izzy's stomach dropped like a fishing weight.

They are both so mad, they can't even sit near me, she thought.

She watched Zelda sip from her water bottle when Taylor sipped from hers. She watched Zelda laugh when Taylor thought something was funny.

She tried to look away, focusing instead on her peanut butter and Fluff. She stared at it as if it was the most interesting thing in the world—as if nothing else existed except that sandwich and the stormy day outside.

Then, as if being pulled by a magnet, her eyes flicked back up. She couldn't stop watching them. Zelda and Piper. Piper and Zelda.

As she watched, she realized that even though Piper sat next to Zelda like she always had, there was something different too. Piper wasn't sipping when Zelda sipped . . . and she wasn't laughing when Zelda thought something was funny.

At that very moment, Piper turned and their eyes met. Izzy wanted to look away, but she couldn't. Piper's mouth opened. Then shut.

Piper got up from the table and began to gather her

uneaten lunch. When she headed toward the garbage cans, Zelda called after her. But Piper didn't stop. Instead, she threw away her lunch, and walked out of the cafeteria alone.

That's when Izzy realized Piper wasn't acting angry. She was acting guilty.

Izzy stared at her own uneaten lunch. Then, as if clicking play on a YouTube video, Tuesday's cafeteria scene began to run through Izzy's brain. In her mind's eye, she watched—as if it was happening right in front of her:

Sitara enters the cafeteria, finds Izzy, and smiles. Apollo is behind her, his hand reaching.

Wait. Pause. Rewind farther back.

Izzy races into the cafeteria to talk to the Sea Stars before Sitara gets there.

Pause. Slow motion.

Izzy is standing in front of Zelda.

But Zelda isn't looking at her.

She's looking around her.

Forward. Pause.

Zelda leans closer to Piper.

Zelda whispers something to Piper that Izzy can't hear.

But Izzy did hear.

At the time, she'd pretended she hadn't heard. She had tried to ignore what she knew Zelda had said—and what it meant.

Pause. Rewind. Play.

"Watch this," Zelda had said.

After school, Izzy purposely missed her bus.

As she made her way to the girls' locker room, she slung her bag over her shoulder. The door shut behind her, its noise ricocheting off the tile walls. The place was empty except for Piper, who was shoving her gym bag into a locker. Izzy stood behind her. Waiting.

"Izzy?" Piper jumped when she noticed her. "You scared me. What are you doing here?"

"I have to ask you a question, Piper."

Piper sat on the bench, picked up her cleats, and began working out a knot in the laces.

A group of girls wearing blue-and-white pinnies and carrying soccer balls ran by. "Hey, Piper, you ready?" one of them called.

"Go ahead," Piper yelled back. "I'll be right out."

"Hurry up!" The girls disappeared through the outside door.

Piper continued to work on her laces.

Izzy crossed her arms. "You need to tell me, Piper."

Piper seemed to freeze for a second, then continued. "Tell you what?"

"In the cafeteria when Apollo pulled off Sitara's hijab. You and Zelda . . . you knew what he was going to do before he did it."

Piper swallowed hard. "No, we didn't."

"Don't lie, Piper."

Piper spun around. "Lie? Ha! You should talk about lying."

"What's that supposed to mean?"

"Do you even care about the Sea Stars anymore, Izzy?"

Izzy blinked. "Of course I do."

Piper stared at her cleats. "Zelda says she told you about how I got grounded that night we waited for you at Brogee's. She says you didn't care."

"I—I cared. But it wasn't my fault. My dad wouldn't let me go and he took away my—"

Piper fixed her gaze on Izzy. "You never said you were sorry."

"You never told me you got grounded."

Piper shook her head. "Zelda's right. You never would have skipped out on us before Sitara showed up."

"She lives with me, Pipe. What am I supposed to do? Ignore her? Plus she's really nice if you just got to—"

"Just got to what, Izzy? Visit? Come see your new house and new room? Spend time with you?"

"You don't understand, Piper." Izzy bit her lip. "That has nothing to do with Sitara."

The outside door opened and a woman popped her head in. "Grenier! You're late. Come on!"

"That's my coach. I gotta go." Piper stood and walked toward the door, carrying her knotted cleats.

"Piper, wait." Izzy stood. "You have to tell me. Was it only Zelda who got Apollo to pull off Sitara's hijab? Or were you in on it too?"

Piper held on to the door handle but didn't budge. "It was a joke, Izzy. It was *supposed* to be a joke."

"Did it seem funny to you?"

Piper looked up and Izzy could see that she had tears in her eyes. "Please don't say anything, Izzy."

Izzy's mouth fell open. It had only been a suspicion—until now.

Apollo might have done the pulling, but Zelda and Piper were just as guilty.

Piper fixed her gaze on Izzy. "If you still care about the Sea Stars, Izzy, you won't say anything. You'll just . . ." Piper's words drifted.

"Just what?"

"You'll forget about it, Izzy. You'll pretend it never happened." Piper shook her head. "I gotta go," she said before ducking outside.

Izzy watched the door close behind her, wondering who that girl was, because she couldn't be her best friend Piper. She was just some girl in stocking feet. Some girl she didn't even know.

Fifth Grade

The summer before fifth grade was the first time our parents let us ride our bikes all the way to the Coffee Cabinet on our own. It was the Fourth of July and the place was packed with surfers and tourists.

The shop was famous for making the best coffee cabinet in all of Rhode Island—a combination of ice cream, milk, and coffee syrup, all blended into a delicious milkshake. Whenever we ordered one, Zelda, Piper, and I pretended it was real coffee.

That day, hot and sweaty from the bike ride, I couldn't wait to taste that first frosty, sweet, and bitter coffee cabinet of summer.

Zelda had another idea.

As we stood in line she said, "I'm getting real coffee," loud enough to make sure a group of teenage girls in bikini tops and jean shorts could hear.

Piper and I stared at her. Our parents would never let us drink real coffee.

"What'll it be?" a boy asked. He had long, dark braids and a name tag that read MALIK.

"Skinny grande iced caramel macchiato."

"Name?" he asked.

Zelda winked. "Beyoncé."

He shook his head but wrote Beyoncé in Sharpie across a cup.

Piper could barely talk, she was giggling so hard. "Same," she said. "For, um . . . Ariana."

Malik rolled his eyes. Then he turned to me. "What'll it be?" he asked.

Zelda nudged me. "Do it," she said. "My mom gets them all the time. They are sooooo good."

"I thought we were getting coffee cabinets?"

"Milkshakes are so fourth grade, Izzy," Zelda said. She put an arm around me but spoke to Malik. "Katy here will have a skinny grande iced caramel macchiato."

Malik looked at me. He had long eyelashes and a nice smile.

I didn't want a macchiato, and I didn't want to be Katy.

Malik tilted his head, giving me that smile again.

"What do you really want?" he asked.

I looked at Zelda and sighed.

"What she said."

Chapter 18

Izzy stumbled outside. Although the rain had stopped, the sky remained dark and gray. The wind kicked up in a fierce gust, spinning the newly fallen leaves in mini tornadoes.

As Izzy pulled out her phone to call her dad, a pack of girls sprinted past. She looked up to see the cross-country team doing their long run. She put the phone away.

Girls kept coming up the hill—a stampede of runners breathing hard. Izzy scanned each face, searching for only one. Just as she thought they'd all passed, she found her.

Red-faced and sweaty, Zelda clutched her side as she trudged up the hill alone. Izzy watched her limp to the other side. Then she took off after her.

The wind whipped her hair and her patchwork bag slapped Izzy's side as she raced to catch up with Zelda. When she was directly behind her, she yelled, "I know what you did!"

Zelda flinched. But she didn't turn around. Instead, she let go of her side and started to jog again.

Izzy sped up, keeping pace. "She never did anything to you!"

Zelda ran faster. "I . . . have no idea . . . what you're talking about," she said between heavy breaths.

Izzy sprinted in front of her so that Zelda had barely enough time to stop before they collided.

"Hey!" Zelda yelled.

The wind gusted.

"You need to tell the truth," Izzy said.

Zelda leaned forward, placing her hands on her knees. "I'm in the middle of cross-country practice, in case you didn't notice."

"You told Apollo to pull off Sitara's hijab. *You* did it.

And if you don't admit it, I'm . . . I'm . . . going to—"
Izzy started.

Zelda fixed her dark green eyes on Izzy. "You're
going to what? Wet your pants and wait for me to
save you? Hide behind a computer? Disappear in your
new house with your new best friend?" Her words cut
sharp as a knife. "You're not going to do anything,
Izzy, because you never do."

Izzy took a step back.

Zelda advanced. "You want to talk about telling the
truth, Izzy? What about you?"

Izzy swallowed hard. "I didn't lie."

"Oh yeah? What about your mom? How about the
fact that you told Piper and me we couldn't come over
because you were going to be at Block Island all weekend when really you were home making your stupid
maps with your new best friend Sitara?"

"What?"

"Really, Izzy—if you're going to blow us off, at least
you can be honest about it. How do you think I felt in
science watching you brag about your great day on the
pond with Sitara after you lied to us?"

Izzy felt as if she'd been stung by a bee.

Zelda leaned so close Izzy could feel her heat. "Best friends don't lie. They tell each other everything," she said. "But I guess you have a new best friend to share your secrets with."

"I don't have secrets."

"Oh, come on, Izzy. Everyone knows your mother never moved home. Everyone knows that she's *never* coming home."

Tears welled in Izzy's eyes. "You knew? And you didn't say anything?"

Zelda sighed. "Look," she said. "You might not like what we did, but it solved everything, didn't it? Sitara quit, right? And that was her choice." She took a breath. "Now we can go back to the way things were— you, me, and Piper. The Sea Stars."

Their eyes met and a lifetime of memories flooded Izzy.

It's Zelda, Izzy reminded herself. *Zelda who helped me stop crying on the first day of kindergarten. Zelda who saved my life in first grade. Zelda who always got me the best birthday presents and who's kept the Sea Stars together, no matter what.*

"Best friends forever," Izzy whispered.

Zelda grinned. "You wanted me to fix things all along, Izzy. Just like always. Some things really don't ever change." She rolled her eyes. "My parents weren't going to let me sleep over at your house, anyway, with those people living upstairs. Plus, the way your dad's been all weird since . . . well, you know."

"What?"

"But I told them it was fine. Even though I didn't want to hang out with Sitara, I said I wanted to stay over anyway because you were still my best friend."

"What do you mean *those people*? The Haidarys are the nicest people I've ever met. And what do you mean about the way my dad's been acting? My dad is fine. My dad is great."

Zelda arched her eyebrow, giving her best *Seriously?* look.

Izzy studied Zelda's face. That's when she understood.

"You're scared of her," she said.

"Ha! I'm not scared of *her*!" Zelda's face started to get red all over again.

"You had Apollo pull off her hijab so you could feel bigger."

"What do you mean bigger?"

"But you're not, Zelda. You're small! You'll always be smaller than Sitara!"

In one fell swoop, Zelda yanked Izzy's bag off her shoulder. She reached in and pulled out a summer's worth of the maps and charts and held them in her fist.

"What are you doing? Give me those!" Izzy screamed.

Zelda held her fist in the air. The papers ruffled in the wind.

"It's either her or us, Izzy. Are you going to save the Sea Stars or not? It's your choice."

"Give me my maps!"

"Us or her!" Zelda lifted a finger.

Izzy stood. Frozen.

Then, one by one, Zelda loosened her fingers. The papers fluttered. Izzy leapt for them . . . but it was too late. She watched in horror as a summer of painstaking work floated into the air and tumbled, as if in a hurricane, down the hill.

Tears bubbled in Izzy's eyes, not only because her maps were floating helter-skelter all around her. She cried because of what it meant.

Zelda looked at her empty hand as if even she was surprised by what she'd done. Suddenly, her seaweed-green eyes weren't so fierce. Instead, they were wet with tears. She stared at Izzy, then, without a word, she ran away—down the hill to where the cross-country team was stretching.

Izzy darted after a paper that had fallen into a puddle. As she pulled it out, the page ripped.

She chased another as it floated toward the woods, but it stuck high in a branch. One flew into the fence. Others littered the damp hill.

Izzy began to cry. She cried for her lost work, but mostly she cried because it was over. The thing she'd feared the most had happened. The Sea Stars were gone.

Izzy fell backward, sitting down hard on the muddy hill.

She could hear the cross-country team doing their spirit cheer, and soccer players calling to each other to pass the ball. Izzy ignored it all, instead burying her head inside her folded arms. Mud seeped into her jeans as tears ran down her face.

She didn't know how long she had sat there crying when she heard a voice.

"These are yours, right?"

Izzy lifted her head.

Roger stood in front of her, holding the maps. She glanced around the hill. It was empty.

Izzy wiped her nose with the back of her hand. "You picked them up?"

Roger was flipping through them. "I never got a chance to see them in science that day. These are really cool." He pointed to one. "Hey, you got the sunken barge on here," he said. "Ha! This is where I dented Skip's prop blade." He smirked. "You better hurry up and finish these before I do it again."

He handed her the maps and she tucked them back inside her bag. "Thank you," she said.

"I heard Zelda saying that stuff." He dug his hands in his pocket. "Skip told me that your mom never came home."

Great, Izzy thought, *even Roger knows.*

He sat next to her. "My mom moved out when I was three." He sniffed. "It sucked at first, but it got better. I visit her in Warwick sometimes."

Izzy stared at him. She hadn't ever thought about Roger having a mom, which of course was stupid. But for as long as she'd known him, it had always been Roger and Skip.

"Where's your friend?" he asked. "You know, the girl who wears the thing on her head . . . Sara, Tara—?"

"Sitara?"

"Yeah."

"It's called a hijab," Izzy said.

"Right. Hijab." Roger picked at the grass. "You know, I never told her, but I thought it was really cool how she talked about all that personal stuff when she did the news that day," he said. "I probably wouldn't have paid attention if I wasn't running the camera, but I thought that was cool the way she explained why she dressed like that. I didn't know it had to do with her religion and stuff." He paused. "I've thought about what she said a lot."

Izzy nodded.

Roger shook his head. "You know, when Apollo pulled off her—"

"Hijab."

"Hijab. Right. I told him that if he ever did anything like that again, I was going to bust him up good. The suspension would seem easy compared to what I was going to do to him."

Izzy smiled. "You did?"

"Yeah, I mean, if Sitara could go in front of the school and talk about all that personal stuff, well . . . I respect that."

Izzy looked away.

"You two are always together. Where is she?"

Izzy didn't even know how to explain it. "At the marina."

"Oh, well, Skip's picking me up . . ." He glanced at his watch. "Thirty minutes ago." He laughed. "Do you want a ride when he finally gets here?"

Izzy nodded.

Roger stood. "Come on," he said. "Let's wait in front."

Riding home with Skip and Roger, Izzy thought about everything that had happened. She thought about how Sitara's speech on TV might not have changed everyone's minds, but it had changed Roger's. And maybe Roger had changed Apollo's—in his own Roger kind of way, anyway.

"You two knuckleheads are lucky I came to get you before it starts storming again," Skip said.

A fierce wind kicked up, sending trees bending and waving in its strong gusts. The gray clouds had turned black.

Unfortunately, the weather wasn't enough of a distraction to keep Zelda's words from bouncing around Izzy's head. *You wanted me to fix things all along, Izzy. Just like always. Some things really don't ever change.*

Is that who I am? Izzy wondered. *The girl who writes the words but is too scared to say them out loud? The girl who hides behind the camera but is too scared to speak into it?*

Maybe Izzy didn't know how to fix things, but she knew who would.

Izzy needed to find her dad.

After Skip dropped her off at the marina, she raced upstairs. "Dad!" she shouted. "Starenka!"

But the apartment was empty.

She thought about going upstairs to see Sitara, but she wasn't ready to face her. First, Izzy had to accept the fact that she was guilty too. She had chosen to ignore Zelda's bullying. She had tried to pretend that it was no big deal—just Zelda being Zelda. *If only I had stood up sooner,* she thought, *maybe none of this would have happened.*

She ran back downstairs, through the yard, around all the boats high and dry on blocks.

"Dad!" she called. She ran into the workshop.

She hadn't been in there since the move. She immediately found her bike, resting against a pile of Mom's stuff.

Izzy froze.

There was something so sad about seeing Mom's things stacked in a crooked pile on the dirty workshop floor.

Mom's sewing machine, which they'd used to make doll clothes, rested against her kneading board and a container full of cookie cutters. Izzy moved the bike to see a clear plastic container of Mom's sweaters and other winter clothes. Izzy suddenly wondered, *Why hasn't Dad put Mom's things away? Why are her clothes still packed as if they're leaving too?*

Izzy ran back outside. "Dad!" she yelled. Then she realized his truck was gone.

She saw Skip heading into the shop. He must have dropped Roger off at home and come back.

"Do you know where my dad is?" she called to him.

"Went to Providence with Hassan. Needed some special part." Skip let the screen door slam hard behind him.

Izzy stood in the middle of the boatyard.

Everyone has abandoned me, she thought.

Thunder rumbled in the distance.

"Where is my family?" she shouted into the black clouds.

A flash of light, followed by a crack of thunder, louder and closer.

"I hate this place!" She was so angry she thought she was going to explode. She ran to the closest boat and kicked the block it rested on. It didn't budge so she did it again.

"I hate you!" she screamed.

She felt as if it was the *Invasion of the Body Snatchers* all over again.

My father is always working. My mother is . . . away. Sitara's barely speaking to me. The Sea Stars . . . She ran up and kicked the boat again. "Gone!" she screamed.

Mom's voice filled her head. *I'm only a boat ride away, Izzy.*

Mom, she thought. Right then, more than anything, Izzy needed her mother. *If I can get to the ferry . . .*

She darted back inside the workshop and wheeled out her bike. The tires were soft, but they'd have to do. Galilee was far, but she knew how to get there. She pulled her cell phone from her back pocket and dialed.

"Loretta's," Mom answered.

As soon as Izzy heard her voice, the tears came. "Mom?"

"Izzy-bug, what's wrong?"

"I'm coming to Block Island."

"Okay," she said. "Let me talk to Dad. I can't do this weekend, but—"

"No, I'm coming right now."

"What are you talking about, honey?"

"I'm going to take the ferry over."

"Izzy, where's Dad?"

"I'm leaving now. I'm taking my bike."

"Sweetheart." Mom paused. "You know you can't ride your bike on Route One. Have you looked outside? It's about to storm and I can't pick you up at Old Harbor right now. I'm in the middle of—"

Izzy swallowed hard. "You're never coming home, are you, Mom?"

"Izzy. I'm—"

"Don't we mean anything to you? I . . . how can

you leave us? How . . ." Her words dissolved in a thick jumble of sobs.

"Izzy, I haven't left you."

"Well, you're not *here*!" Izzy cried. "I need you right now and you're not *here*."

"How about next weekend? You know the Aunts' cottage is small but—"

"No," Izzy said. She felt as though if one more person rejected her, she was going to explode. "Why should I have to go there? You need to move home with Dad and me."

"Izzy, it's not that easy. I have responsibilities here."

"You have responsibilities *here*. Don't you want to be with me?"

"Of course I do." Mom paused. "Honey, are you okay?"

"No," Izzy said. She wanted to hurt her mom as much as she'd hurt her. "Never mind. Stay there. I changed my mind. I don't want you here at all."

Izzy threw the phone as hard as she could. Then she jumped on her bike and started pedaling.

Sixth Grade

I used to wonder what it sounded like when the continents broke apart. I used to think it was a ripping-crashing noise, like the sand an excavator makes when it tears down the house you grew up in.

But now I think it's a quiet sound—as quiet as a Humvee after an explosion. So quiet, you don't even realize it's happening at first. Until all that's left is blood and rubble.

I wonder if that's how Sitara felt when she found out that the Taliban destroyed her home.

I wonder if she had a sticker in her bedroom window, and soft white curtains that floated as light as an ocean breeze.

I wonder if, when she listens real hard, she can hear the sound of her world ripping apart too.

Chapter 19

As thick black thunderclouds scudded across the sky, Izzy coasted down Surfside Avenue. Rain fell in soaking sheets. It was as if she was looking at the world through a dull gray lens. Fortunately, she didn't need to see to know how to get to where she was going.

At the intersection of Rosewood and Moonstone, she hit the brakes. Her back tire skidded out of control as she slammed into the SOLD sign. She found herself face-down on the muddy lawn. Her knee began to bleed.

The excavator stared at her like a threat.

She stood up. "Coward!" she shouted at it.

Rain spilled over the gutters as if the house were crying too. She wondered if it knew—knew that its family was gone, knew that it would be gone soon too.

There wouldn't be any more first-day-of-school waffles at 55 Rosewood Avenue. It would never smell like bait fish or wet dog or sunscreen or hot spinach pies ever again.

In her mind's eye, she could see it all—Dad at the table charting an offshore trip. Mom rolling dough at the counter. Flotsam at her feet.

Izzy dug her hand into her pocket and took out the key. The muddy front lawn tugged at her flip-flops as she slogged toward the front door. She inserted the key and turned it. The door yawned open and Izzy stepped inside.

The stale heat of the house wrapped around her—warm and dry.

The house was the same, but not the same. Telltale signs of their former life were everywhere. Shiny patches of wood floor where the furniture had protected it—sun-bleached and scratched everywhere else.

"Hello!" she yelled. "I'm home."

The wind whistled through cracks, filling its empty corners.

"Don't you miss us?" Izzy shouted.

But the house didn't answer.

Izzy stomped up the stairs, making as much noise as possible. At the top, she opened her old bedroom door, walking straight to the window. She pressed her hand flat against the SAVE THE NARWHALS sticker.

If only there was a sticker that saved families, she thought.

She opened the window and rain blew in. She turned, scanning the room she'd taken for granted. There was still tape on the wall from her *Endless Summer* poster and the hook that used to hold her sea star mobile. One of her hair elastics lay on the ground. She bent down to pick it up, then used it to pull her hair back in a tight ponytail.

She moved to the doorway, touching each mark that Dad had made when he measured her height, the night before every first day of school, then steadied herself against the tide of memories flooding her brain. She sat down hard in the middle of the floor and hugged her knees, making her body small against the gusting wind. The curtains blew in and out, as if the room it-self was breathing.

It would never be the same again.

Suddenly she was so tired. She was tired of the marina and tired of school. She was tired of trying to keep the Sea Stars together. And tired of watching them fall apart. She closed her eyes and let her body rock. Back and forth. Ebb and flow. *This is better*, she thought. *Darkness. Escape.* She let everything go.

When she was too tired to even rock anymore, she stretched out on her side. It wasn't long before she fell asleep.

A rumbling sound woke Izzy. Her eyes popped open.

Someone somewhere was shouting.

"Stop!" The voice was coming from outside.

Izzy sat up, rubbing her arm where she'd slept on it. How long had it been? *Five minutes? Fifty?*

The voice again. This time louder. "My daughter might be in there!"

The rumbling sound cut.

"Izzy!"

"Mom?"

Izzy tried to stand, but the left side of her body felt

like pins and needles. She sat back down hard and rubbed her arm.

Suddenly Mom burst into the room. "Izzy!" she shouted. She began to run toward her, but then flew to the window and stuck her head out. "She's here, Vince. I found her!"

Izzy could hear the front door bang open downstairs. Her father's footsteps thundered up the stairs as Mom gathered her in a tight hug.

Dad bolted into the room. "Izzy!" he breathed. "Are you okay?"

"She's okay, Vince. She's okay," her mother said between sobs.

Even though she thought she couldn't possibly have any tears left, Izzy broke down all over again as her father knelt and wrapped his arms around her and her mother.

"Dad," Izzy finally said. "You're squishing me."

He let go. Mom wiped Izzy's tears with the sleeve of her flannel shirt.

"Mom, how did you get here?" Izzy asked.

"When you hung up, I drove to Old Harbor. I had missed the ferry, but I told Pete it was an emergency. Turns out the *Flying Glass* really can fly." She smiled through her tears. "He brought me to the marina. Dad and I have been driving around looking for you."

Izzy hung her head. "I'm sorry. How did you know I was here?"

"I told Skip," Dad said. "Roger called me to say he saw your bike in front of the house."

"We were so worried, Izzy," Mom said.

"I . . . I wanted to see it one more time before it's . . . gone."

Mom bit her lip. "Well, you were almost gone with it, sweetheart. When the rain stopped, the guys came back to the excavators. They were about to tear the house down."

Izzy started crying all over again. "I thought if I came here, everything would go back to the way it was." Her eyes flitted back and forth between her father and mother. "You have to tell me the truth. Are you getting divorced?"

Her mother's gaze met her father's and then she took Izzy's hand in hers. "The truth is, Izzy, we don't know what's next. We're still figuring it out."

287

"But that doesn't make any of what we shared together in this house less real," Dad said.

Izzy sniffed.

"You know, Izzy, when you came to see me on the island, you didn't let me finish the story about the time we found the sea stars on the beach," Mom said.

"I know how it ends, Mom."

"Let me finish, Izzy," Mom said. "What I was trying to say was that the three of us, we did that together."

Dad took Mom's hand in his. "No matter what happens, Izzy, we're always going to be a team. We're always going to love you. And that's something that's never going to change."

Izzy leaned in, letting her parents hug her.

Outside, as her mom and dad talked to the guy in the excavator, Izzy stared at the tiny blue cottage as if taking a picture with her brain. She wanted to hold on to every detail.

The storm had passed, leaving the air smelling fresh and clean.

The excavator rumbled to life as Dad tossed Izzy's bike onto the back of the truck. "Ready?" he said.

"Wait," Izzy said. "One more minute."

Her parents joined her. Izzy put an arm around each of them. She thought she might cry again, but instead she took a deep breath. It was time to be brave.

"Thank you, home," Mom said.

"Thank you for protecting us against nor'easters," Dad said.

"Thank you for not getting mad when Flotsam scratched your front door when the fireworks scared him on the Fourth of July," Izzy said.

"Thank you for the ocean breeze that came through your windows at night," Mom added.

"And for smelling like spinach pies and bait fish," Dad said.

Mom laughed. "I don't know about the fish."

Izzy gave her parents an extra squeeze.

"Goodbye," she said to the house.

Then she walked past the rumbling excavator and climbed into the cab of her dad's truck.

They drove to Galilee, where Izzy and her dad walked Mom to the ferry.

"Oh, good. You got the *Carol Jean*," Izzy said. "She's my favorite."

Mom grinned. "Mine too."

"So you think there will be room for me on Columbus Day weekend?" Izzy asked.

"I'm sure of it," Mom said.

As Izzy and her father made their way back to the truck, she caught him staring. There at the dock, the *Isabella Rose* bobbed in its slip.

"Pete says he has a buyer who's interested." He shrugged. "She sure was a fine boat."

Izzy nodded, feeling selfish. She hadn't been the only one dealing with change. Her dad had had to leave his fishing business, but he never complained. Instead he put his energy into the marina.

On the ride home, Izzy thought about that. She thought about Starenka's family learning to run a farm in a new country. She thought about Mom learning how to run a restaurant.

And Sitara.

She thought about the many goodbyes Sitara had had to say in the last year. Izzy knew that what she had lost was nothing compared to what Sitara had been through. But Sitara never complained. She was ready to take on every challenge, and hurdle every obstacle. She was Maria Bashir. She wouldn't let the enemy destroy her.

Until they did.

Over the last year Izzy realized how she'd chosen to bury her head in the sand instead of facing the truth. It was easy to pretend that her lies to Zelda and Piper about her mom had been innocent. But she was starting to realize that no lie really is. She hadn't accepted the truth about her parents or middle school. And no matter how many times her father tried to talk to her about what had happened in Afghanistan, she refused to listen.

Most of all, she hadn't wanted to be honest about the Sea Stars, especially how Zelda had treated Sitara.

Starenka's words filled Izzy's head. *Is your fear bigger than your courage or is your courage bigger than your fear?*

Izzy decided that it was time to find out.

"Dad," she said. "I want to hear what happened in Afghanistan. I want to hear everything."

Chapter 20

When they got back to the marina, it was too late for Izzy to talk to Sitara. But that was okay; she needed more time to work out her plan.

The next morning she explained what she wanted to do to her dad. He nodded solemnly as he sipped his coffee. "I'll talk to Hassan today," he said. Then he gave her a hug. "I'm proud of you, Izzy-bug."

At school, Izzy entered the tech ed room. At first she was worried about facing Zelda and Piper, but they both seemed to hide in the control room, as if they were more worried about seeing Izzy than she was about seeing them.

Mr. Cantor leaned over Roger, who was tinkering with camera B. "Skip thought maybe if I get this piece soldered it will work. He said he can help."

Izzy focused her gaze on Mr. Cantor's fluorescent orange bow tie. The angry-ocean sound began a low roar. Izzy took a deep breath and did her best to ignore it. "Mr. Cantor?" she said.

He looked up. "Miss Mancini." He removed his glasses and squinted as if making sure it was really her addressing him.

"Um, can I talk to you for a minute?" she asked. "Privately."

That afternoon, Izzy raced home from the bus stop. As she entered their apartment, Starenka was asleep at the kitchen table. A scratchy baseball game played on her transistor. Izzy tiptoed past her and into her bedroom. She scanned her bookshelf until she found the weathered green leather binding. She grabbed the book and made her way back through the kitchen, opening the door as quietly as possible.

"Ack!" Starenka said, sitting up. "They look for you all night and now you are disappearing all over again?"

"I'm going upstairs to see Sitara."

"Ack!" she heard her say again as Izzy shut the door behind her.

Izzy took the stairs two at a time. She knocked and opened the door. Her dad sat at the kitchen table drinking chai with the Haidarys.

Izzy stood frozen in the doorway, her gaze darting from her dad to Mrs. Haidary to Dr. Haidary, silently asking the question that she knew her father had already asked.

Mrs. Haidary nodded.

"Yes, yes, of course." Dr. Haidary said. "How can I ever say no to your father? Sitara is in her bedroom. She is the one you really need to ask."

Izzy's face broke into a giant smile. "Manana!" she said. "Thank you!"

At Sitara's door, Izzy knocked.

The door opened. "Izzy!" Sitara leapt up, gathering her in a hug. "Are you okay? Baba and I were looking for you last night. We came home when your dad called to say he found you."

"I'm fine." Izzy closed the door behind her.

"Where did you go?"

Izzy looked at the book in her hands. "Home."

Sitara's forehead wrinkled. "I don't understand. Your home is here."

"I went to my old house—the one I lived in with my dad *and* my mom before we moved here."

"Were you looking for something?"

"Kind of . . . I guess I thought that by going there I could turn back time or something and make everything go back to the way it was."

Sitara nodded as if she understood.

"But it doesn't work that way. You can't stop things from changing by pretending they're not. I get that now." She looked up at Sitara.

"I'm sorry, Izzy."

"It's okay," Izzy said. "Actually, it's more than okay. Going there helped me figure out a lot of stuff."

"What?"

"That no matter how much everything around you changes, the people who love you don't."

Sitara smiled. "I like that."

"Me too." Izzy grinned. "Anyway, I brought you a present."

Sitara looked up. "For me?"

"Yes, you. But don't get too excited. It used to be mine."

"That makes it even better," Sitara said.

Izzy started to hand her the book, then pulled it back. "I'm only giving it to you on one condition."

"What?"

"You do the news with me tomorrow."

Sitara's smile faded. "I can't. I don't go to school there anymore."

"You can. My dad's already talked to your parents and they say, yes, and . . . ," Izzy paused. "I talked to Mr. Cantor today. He scheduled us to anchor tomorrow."

"You asked Mr. Cantor?" Sitara raised her eyebrows. "You said you would never do the news on camera."

"That was before."

"Before what?"

"Before you. Until you went with me through the breachway, I was too afraid to go into the ocean. You helped me remember how much I loved it." Izzy grinned. "Sitara, you are the bravest person I know. If you can come to a new country and overcome all the bad stuff you've had to deal with while staying *you*—well, I should be able to face hard stuff too."

Pink crept across Sitara's cheeks as she tried not to smile. "So, what's the present?" she finally asked.

Izzy held out the book. "It's *The Lion, the Witch and the Wardrobe*. From the Chronicles of Narnia," she said. "Remember how I said going up on the roof was like traveling to Narnia?"

"Yes," Sitara replied.

"Narnia was a magical place, but bad stuff happened there too. It was only when Lucy and her siblings stood up to the evil that it became beautiful again."

Sitara accepted the book. Her fingers brushed the image of Lucy and Susan riding on the back of the lion, Aslan. "It's perfect."

"Please do the news with me, Sitara. I can't do it without you."

"Well," Sitara said. "You do need me. I mean, how are you getting into your locker without me there?"

Izzy grinned. "You'll do it?"

Sitara nodded, then her face got serious. "But what if . . . what if the bad stuff happens again?"

"Don't worry. I know what to do."

The next morning, Izzy's father and Dr. and Mrs. Haidary drove Izzy and Sitara to Shoreline Regional Middle School.

Mrs. Haidary wore a long dark-blue dress and matching hijab, trimmed with pearls and beads.

"Khaista," Izzy said, remembering the Pashto word for *beautiful*.

"Thank you," Mrs. Haidary replied.

Mr. Cantor was waiting for them, wearing a bow tie that had red and white stripes on one side and white stars set on a blue background on the other. He welcomed everyone as they entered the tech ed room.

Zelda was busy scanning the assignment board. "Why is Izzy on anchor?" she said to Mr. Cantor, as if Izzy wasn't standing right there. "She doesn't do the news. She's too—"

"Actually, I do." Izzy headed toward the anchor table, then paused, turning to face Zelda. "By the way, Zelda," she began. "You know the question you asked me the other day?"

Zelda's forehead wrinkled.

"I just want you to know . . ." Izzy took a deep breath. "I choose Sitara."

Zelda's mouth fell open, but before she could make a sound, Mr. Cantor shouted, "Places, everyone!" To the parents, he said, "Why don't you stand right here with me?"

"Hi, Zelda. Hi, Piper," Izzy's dad said as the girls made their way to the control room.

"Hi, Mr. Mancini," Piper replied shyly. Zelda walked past without a word.

"Are you scared?" Sitara whispered to Izzy.

"Terrified," she said, swallowing hard. "But someone once told me that being brave is the same thing."

Sitara nodded.

Roger walked over. "Hey, I actually fixed camera B, so I can have a camera on each of you today."

"You did?" Izzy said. "That's great!"

Roger shrugged. "Skip helped me. Guess I'm good at fixing stuff like my dad."

As the room got quiet, the angry-ocean sound began to churn in Izzy's ears. *Not now*, she told it. Then she remembered what her father had said about going through the breachway. *You can do it, Iz. Just remember . . . stay in front of the current. If you're faster . . . you're in control. If you're slower, then it's in control of you.* Izzy knew then—she needed to stay in front of her fear. It was the same as the advice Starenka had shared on the dock that night.

My courage is bigger than my fear, she reminded herself.

"Everyone ready? Here we go," Mr. Cantor said as he straightened his star-spangled bow tie.

Roger got into position behind the cameras. Mr. Cantor held up his hand. "Five, four . . ." He counted down on his fingers: *three, two, one.*

Roger flicked the switch and both camera lights turned green.

"Good morning. Today is Friday, September fourteenth, and this is your Shoreline Regional Middle School news," Sitara said.

Right then, Izzy couldn't see anything except the green lights. She opened her mouth, but nothing came out.

Mr. Cantor rotated his finger as if to say, *Camera's rolling!*

But it didn't matter. Izzy's words seemed to disappear in the growing sound of the ocean that filled her ears.

That's when Mrs. Haidary stepped forward. She fixed her gaze on Izzy, just as she had done in her kitchen that afternoon. She nodded firmly, then lifted her chin high. And even though she didn't say one word, Izzy understood her loud and clear: *You can do this.*

Izzy nodded back, then took a deep breath. The angry-ocean sound disappeared. "Today is National Cream-Filled Donut Day," she said.

"Lunch is grilled cheese sandwiches," Sitara said. "Sadly, no donuts."

Izzy felt her shoulders loosen. "There is a soccer game at three o'clock in the lower field. Go Stingrays!"

"On this day in history, in 1814," Sitara began, "Francis Scott Key wrote the poem 'The Defense of Fort McHenry.'"

Izzy continued, "He was inspired to see the flag still flying over the fort after a night of fighting and bombing."

"Mr. Key's poem became the words of the national anthem of the United States of America, 'The Star-Spangled Banner,'" Sitara said.

Izzy's face got serious. "I think that story about our national anthem and the words 'our flag was still there' are

perfect for what Sitara and I want to talk about today."
She looked straight into the camera. "My friend Sitara is
a lot like our flag. No matter all the bad stuff she's been
through, she never gives up—she's still standing. She's
taught me a lot about what it means to be brave."

Sitara smiled. "Thanks, Izzy. Any courage I have
comes from my parents," she said. "Most of us would
rather not think about what happens far away."

"But on January seventh of this year, while on a
mission for the war in Afghanistan, a vehicle drove
straight into the Humvee that my father and Sitara's
father, Dr. Haidary, were driving," Izzy said.

"It was what they call a VBIED—a vehicle-borne
improvised explosive device. The Taliban had filled a
car with explosives. When it hit the Humvee, they
detonated it," Sitara said.

"The explosion caused my father to become partially
paralyzed. He also suffered injuries like post-traumatic
stress disorder, or PTSD. An injury that no one can see
but can be life-threatening just the same." Izzy took a
deep breath. "The only reason he is still here is because
Dr. Haidary saved his life," she continued. "We are telling you about this because we want you to remember the

approximately one point four million men and women who, each day, risk their lives for our country and for us—including those who have never been to the United States, like Dr. Haidary at the time of that attack."

"Some people see that I dress differently and wear hijab, and they make up their minds about who they think I am based on that," Sitara said. "But they don't know anything about me, or my family, or the things we've been through. They don't understand that the war they have seen only on TV, we have seen with our own eyes. They don't know the things my father has sacrificed for our freedom and for yours."

"Sometimes," Izzy continued, "the truth isn't easy to see. Sometimes you have to look below the surface to find it."

"So instead of judging people by how they look on the outside, we wanted to make up a symbol we can use to let each other know that we care—especially for all the stuff you might be dealing with on the inside that no one else can see. It's a way to say, 'I believe in you,' and to show support," Sitara said.

The girls each held up their right hands. "You start with a peace sign." The girls made their fingers form a V.

"Then cross your middle and index fingers, making your fingers come together like in an X," Sitara said.

"We came up with it as a symbol to show unity—you know, like everyone coming together," Izzy said.

"No one can know what someone else is going through by judging them from the outside."

"But we can all be kind to show we support each other on the inside."

The girls held up their crossed fingers.

"My name is Sitara Haidary."

"And my name is Izzy Mancini."

"And this is your Shoreline Regional Middle School news," they said together.

"That's a cut!" Mr. Cantor said.

The camera went dark.

Izzy and Sitara high-fived before removing their mics and joining their parents and Mr. Cantor.

"In all my years as a journalist, I think that was the best news I've ever heard," he said, turning to their parents. "You must be very proud."

Dr. and Mrs. Haidary beamed at Sitara.

Izzy's dad put his hand on Izzy's shoulder. "Every day."

Chapter 21

For the whole next week, Izzy and Sitara took turns swapping with Roger and Nathaniel to write script, anchor the news, and operate the cameras.

Zelda acted as if Izzy didn't exist and Piper continued to follow Zelda around as if there were an invisible rope tying them together.

But good things happened too. Izzy saw kids give each other the unity sign in hallways and on the bus. And lots of kids introduced themselves to Sitara and asked her and Izzy to sit with them at lunch.

One afternoon, as they sat with a new group in the

cafeteria, Izzy watched Piper and Zelda hanging on the fringe of Taylor's table. "I can't lie," Izzy confided in Sitara one day. "I do miss them, even after what they did. We've been friends for a long time. It's hard to just walk away."

Sitara shook her head. "If only Zelda had told me she was sorry, maybe I could forgive her," she said. "But I don't think she'll ever be big enough to do that."

Even though Izzy knew the Sea Stars were over, she wasn't going to let that interfere with her love of all things hidden beneath the ocean, so on that following Friday, when she and Sitara were anchoring the news, she decided to include a new sea star question.

Smiling into the camera, Sitara asked, "If a group of sharks is called a shiver . . ."

"And a group of whales is called a pod . . . ," Izzy added.

"And a group of stingrays is called a fever . . ."

"What is a group of sea stars called?" Izzy asked. Listen Monday to hear the right answer."

"My name is Sitara Haidary."

"And my name is Izzy Mancini."

"This has been your Shoreline Regional Middle School news."

That afternoon, when Izzy came home from school, she found a present on the kitchen table with her name on it.

"Where did this come from?" she asked Dad.

"Mrs. Haidary brought it down while you were at school. I think Sitara wanted to surprise you."

Izzy removed the wrapping paper to find a hard-cover notebook with the image of a giant wave on the front. She opened it. The pages were empty, except for a handwritten note on the inside cover: *Dear Izzy, When I write down my thoughts and feelings, it helps me find courage that I didn't know I had. I hope it will help you too, even though I know that you are already very brave. From your friend, Sitara.*

Izzy thought about everything that had happened. She thought about Zelda and Piper and how they first met. She thought about truth and courage—and how sometimes you had to look below the surface to find it. Then she took the notebook into her room.

She grabbed a pen from her bag and flopped onto her bed. She put the pen to paper and she began to write the first words in her brand-new journal: *If you asked Zelda, she'd tell you that she invented the Sea Stars . . .*

That night, Sitara and Izzy sat on the roof, looking for shooting stars.

Izzy zipped up her hoodie as dried leaves skittered across the roof.

The next day was Saturday, September twenty-second, the official last day of summer, and Izzy knew that they probably wouldn't be visiting Narnia much more until next summer.

"We should have a party," Sitara said. "To celebrate."

"To celebrate what?" Izzy made a sad face. "Being cold? Wait until it's January and you can see your breath on the way to the bus stop. You'll be crying about the end of summer then."

Sitara nudged Izzy. "You must remember, my friend. With every end, there is a new beginning."

Izzy rolled her eyes. "You're a poet now too?"

Sitara laughed.

"Who would we invite to a party?" Izzy asked.

"Everyone," Sitara said. "Our families and—I don't know—friends?"

Izzy frowned. Friends. As horrible as Piper and Zelda had been, the thought of never talking to them again still made her stomach hurt. Once upon a time they had been the Sea Stars. Once upon a time they had been magic.

As if Sitara could read Izzy's thoughts, she turned to her. "Piper wrote me a very kind apology letter. I can tell she's really sorry."

"And Zelda?" Izzy asked.

Sitara held her sweatshirt tight around her neck. "I'm still angry with her, but the Qur'ân reminds me to forgive. Sometimes that means taking the first step."

"So you're going to forget about it like it never happened?"

"No. I won't forget. But maybe we can start again."

"I don't know," Izzy said.

The hurt she felt from what had happened was kind of like the wrinkles in her maps after Zelda had tossed them into the wind. No matter how hard she had tried to smooth out the creases, they wouldn't go away. Now there were wrinkles in their friendship too.

"Maybe you're right," Izzy said. "Instead of running away from change, maybe we should welcome it with a party."

Sitara clapped. "Yes! Can we make invitations?"

Izzy smiled back. "Invitations would be perfect."

Chapter 22

On Saturday morning, Izzy rode her bike around town, delivering invitations to their "Welcome, Change!" party at Brogee's.

That evening, her dad built a giant bonfire on the beach while Dr. and Mrs. Haidary unpacked enough food to feed an army.

Hikmat and Ali took turns throwing a tennis ball into the ocean for Flotsam to fetch, while Starenka sat in a beach chair with her transistor radio listening to the Sox beat San Francisco.

"Ack!" she said. "Tony Macaroni's gonna owe me money!"

Skip and Roger came with a bushel of quahogs and all the fixings to make s'mores. Roger even made Skip take him to a special shop in Kingston to make sure the marshmallows were halâl. Izzy had to keep an eye on Hikmat and Ali so they didn't feed any more to Flotsam, who wore a suspiciously sticky sand mustache.

"What's that?" Hikmat asked, pointing at the concrete structure on the beach.

"Cool!" Ali said.

Izzy stared at the Sea Star Headquarters. It looked so small, she was surprised she'd ever been able to fit inside.

"That . . . ," Izzy said, "is your new clubhouse."

Ali climbed on top, then shimmied down through the hole in the roof. His face peeked out the square window in front. "This is awesome!" he yelled. "Come on, Hikmat!"

Sitara was busy laying blankets on the beach so they could watch for falling stars when it got dark.

Izzy couldn't stop herself from glancing into the parking lot to see if anyone else was coming.

As the sun fell below the horizon, Izzy scanned Block Island. Searching . . . and then a flash.

Izzy smiled. "Blink . . . one . . . two . . . three . . . four . . . blink," she said.

She put her hand to her sea star necklace as she thought about Mom, sleeves rolled up at Loretta's Kitchen. Earlier, Mom had called to let her know that she'd cleared Columbus Day weekend for them to spend together. They'd ride their bikes around the island, drink coffee cabinets, and eat spinach pies. Izzy couldn't wait.

Sitara plopped down next to Izzy. "I have found my new favorite food," she said as she bit into her fourth s'more.

"I'll have to introduce you to peanut butter and Fluff," Izzy said.

"They have halâl Fluff?" Sitara said, laughing.

"They should!" Izzy grinned.

The friends leaned back on their elbows, digging their feet into the cool sand. The Atlantic Ocean rolled out in front of them—impossibly big.

Right then, Izzy thought about Marie Tharp and the ocean and her dedication to uncovering the secrets it hid. Even when she wasn't allowed to go on the research vessels, Marie Tharp didn't accept what other scientists had said. They had made guesses by looking at the surface of the ocean. Marie Tharp chose to look deeper. In so doing, she discovered the truth and changed the minds of people around the world.

Izzy turned toward Sitara, who seemed to be trying to look clear across the ocean. Sitara didn't need to say out loud what she was looking for. Izzy already knew.

"Do you think you'll ever go back?" Izzy asked.

"Yes," Sitara said. "Maybe we'll go together."

"I'd like that," Izzy said. "But only if you take me to the best qabuli palaw restaurant in Afghanistan."

Sitara laughed. "You already ate there," she said. "No one cooks like Mor."

Right then, Flotsam ran toward the parking lot and started barking. Someone else had arrived. But it was too dark to see who.

"Hey, puppy," a voice said. "I've missed you."

"They're over there on the blankets," Izzy heard her dad say.

Izzy watched a light bobbing toward them like a lightning bug. She got up and walked toward it until she found herself standing alone with Piper.

Izzy dug her hands in her pockets. "You came," she said.

"Thanks for the invite."

Izzy looked past her to see if there was anyone else.

Piper shook her head. "I called Zelda to see if she'd come with me. I guess she isn't ready yet."

Izzy nodded.

"But I am." Piper's eyebrows furrowed. "I apologized to Sitara, but I haven't to you, Izzy. I want you to know I'm really sorry."

A soft breeze blew off the ocean, making Izzy feel so light she thought that if she stretched out her arms, she'd rise into the sky just like the seagulls on the pond. A smile spread across her face. "Magic mërghëy," she said.

"What?" Piper asked.

"Oh, nothing." Izzy couldn't stop grinning. "I'm just so glad you're here, Pipe."

Piper grinned back. "Me too."

"Come on." Izzy nodded toward the blankets. "Sitara's over here."

As they approached, Sitara was licking marshmallow from her fingers. "Piper, you should have a s'more! They are soooooo good!"

Just then, Flotsam galloped past with Hikmat and Ali in pursuit. Both boys' faces were covered in chocolate, and Izzy was pretty sure Ali had the last bag of marshmallows tucked under his arm.

The girls laughed. "Um, I don't think there's any left," Piper said as she and Izzy settled onto the blanket next to Sitara.

"There's supposed to be a meteor shower tonight," Sitara said. "Maybe we'll see a shooting star."

For a while there was no sound except the crash of waves.

"I liked your sea star question on the news yesterday," Piper said. "Remember the sea star tank Mrs. Robert set up on our first day of kindergarten?"

"Of course." Izzy grinned. "It's where we first met."

Piper nodded. "So does that mean you finally found out what a group of sea stars is called?"

"I think so," Izzy said.

"So what is it?" Piper asked.

Izzy stared into the sky. "A galaxy," she said. "A galaxy of sea stars."

"Perfect," Sitara said, grinning.

Izzy knew then that even though she and Sitara were born on opposite sides of the world, they were the same too. Sitara was like a star up in the heavens, shiny and bright, while Izzy was comfortably quiet below the sea. Together, they made up their own unique galaxy.

Izzy also knew that she would never again limit herself to anything smaller than a galaxy. Not a posse or flock or gaggle or pack. Not a swarm or herd or gang. From now on, only a galaxy would be big enough for her.

Impossibly big.

"If it's okay with both of you, I'd really like to be part of your galaxy," Piper said.

Even in the dark, Izzy could tell she was smiling. "There's plenty of room," she said.

Suddenly there was a whoop of laughter from the adults huddled around the bonfire.

Izzy cupped her hands around her mouth and shouted, "Roger! Come over here with us! We're looking for the last falling star of summer!"

Roger walked over, his hands jammed in his pockets. "It's freezing over here," he said. "Why don't you guys come by the fire?"

"It's not so bad," Izzy said as she made room for him. "Squeeze in."

He brushed his long, dark bangs off his face before plopping down between Izzy and Sitara. "I don't know if I want to see the last falling star of summer," he said. "I've never liked endings."

"Don't worry, Roger," Izzy said. "It's only the beginning."

Author's Note

I grew up with the stories of my grandparents—
immigrants from then Austria-Hungary—who
came to a country that did not welcome them with
open arms. Even as an old woman, my grandmother often recounted stories of discrimination,
as if still trying to make sense of a world that
often judged her by her accent before her ability.

My grandmother's stories—some of which I've
retold through the voice of Izzy's grandmother,
Starenka—have stayed with me. Starenka's
mother's experience crossing the Atlantic in steerage, as well as the burning of her family's milk

house, was inspired by accounts relayed to me by my grandmother and others.

I do not share my grandparent's stories to compare them to anyone else's. Clearly, others have faced far worse treatment. My point is that my grandparents were not unlike countless other immigrants who have faced persecution in the United States. So, today, when I see religious practices and places of worship desecrated, and families seeking asylum separated at the border, it continues to baffle me how a nation of immigrants can continue to level discrimination on its newest arrivals. I can't help but wonder: Will we, as a nation, ever change?

Perhaps it was this question that guided me to the amazing organization IRIS—Integrated Refugee and Immigrant Services in New Haven, Connecticut (irisct.org). With the help of IRIS, a brilliant and talented group of young women met with me to discuss their experiences coming to the United States as refugees. Over the course of a year, these amazing women from the countries of Afghanistan, Iraq, and Syria read three versions of *A Galaxy of Sea Stars*—each time offering their critical insight and advice and lending their strong voices to help me tell Sitara's story accurately and authentically.

When I asked these ladies if they could go back to when they first came to the United States and had the opportunity to tell their peers something that would have made their transition to America easier, their answer was as simple as it was powerful: "Be kind. You don't know what people have gone through."

Author Vivian Grey, who founded the Rutgers University Council on Children's Literature, has said, "The vision we present to children becomes the future." It is my hope that *Galaxy* might play a small role in amplifying the already strong and powerful voices of immigrants and refugees who, like my grandparents, came to the US with little but a desire to work hard and make a better life.

There is something about being at IRIS and sitting among these phenomenal ladies that is like going home for me. Perhaps it is because when they tell their stories, I hear my grandmother

Iren's voice—except these women tell a different story than my grandmother did. Despite the obstacles they have had to overcome and the challenges they continue to face, these ladies' spirits remain bright with optimism. Like Sitara, they radiate strength and resilience. When I am with them, I am confident that their strong voices will change the narrative of how the United States welcomes refugees. Somehow I know that my grandmother hears them too.

Acknowledgments

I have so much to be grateful for that it is difficult to know where to begin to thank my impossibly big galaxy of friends and family.

Of course there is no one more important in making a book come to life than its editor, and I am so lucky that I get to work with the best. Thank you to the brilliant and kind Janine O'Malley for never faltering in your belief of Izzy's story (or me). Your wisdom and confidence is contagious. Special thanks also to Melissa Warten for her editing skills as well as Rich Deas and Cassie Gonzales for another gorgeous cover. I am forever grateful to be part of the Farrar Straus Giroux galaxy!

My agent Stacey Glick, vice president at Dystel, Goderich & Bourret, who is always there supporting, encouraging, and believing.

My husband, Paul Ferruolo, love of my life and captain of #TeamFerruolo, who I can always count on to bring incredible energy and passion to any adventure—whether it's a four a.m. trip to Killington, the Canyon, or Memorial Sloane Kettering Cancer Center: Thank you for reading numerous drafts of this story to ensure that the explanations of currents, tides, how to drive a boat through the breachway, and all things maritime were accurate. Most of all, thank you for reminding me each day that everything will be okay.

Hilla Nasruddin, Maria Stanekzai, Safia Stanekzai, Asma Rahimyar, Deyana Al-Mashhadani, Nour Al Zouabi—it has been an incredible honor for me to get to know each one of you. My heart swells at least three sizes when we are together. Thank you for sharing your experiences and insights on language, customs, and culture. You brighten the galaxy with your spirit, courage, intelligence, hard work, and persistence. Look out, world—these phenoms dazzle!

My brother, Lieutenant Colonel Robert Zulick (RET), who not only had to deal with the task of growing up with three sisters, but who, for thirty-one years, accepted the challenge to serve his country (not sure which was more difficult). My brother, who did two tours in Afghanistan for Operation Enduring Freedom, is clearly one of our country's bravest and finest. I owe him a huge debt of gratitude for revisiting the difficult details surrounding the Taliban attack on his vehicle while on convoy and for advising me on the likely details surrounding Vince Mancini's story. Any mistakes are my own. I did not fully comprehend or appreciate the risks my brother made serving our country until I interviewed him for this book—a reminder that thanking our nation's veterans is important but actually listening to and hearing their stories is imperative. Thank you, Robert, for sharing yours.

Ashley Makar and Ann O'Brien of IRIS—Integrated Refugee and Immigrant Services (irisct.org) in New Haven, Connecticut, I am quite sure that all of the stars in the galaxy aligned when I met you. Thank you for being so kind and for welcoming me so generously into the IRIS family.

The incredibly talented Bette Anne Rieth, thank you for always being there—reading and providing critical feedback on the many rough drafts of *Galaxy*. Your brilliant insight and ability to hear the heartbeat beneath the words helped me tell Izzy's and Sitara's stories better. I can't wait for the world to read your beautiful books. I will be first in line!

Thank you to Maureen McInerney, Grace McInerney, Mary Ann Cook, and Jill McLaughlin for reading early drafts of *Galaxy* and helping me accurately and authentically describe the unique beauty of the great state of Rhode Island.

Madalyn Stanley, Jennifer Canavan, Chloe Goodin, Anna Bocchino, and Sophia Ferruolo—thank you for reading *Galaxy* and for providing details on how a middle school television news show is produced and what it's like to be a sixth grade girl moving to a regional school. You ladies are rock stars in the galaxy of life.

Ďakujem veľmi pekne to Mrs. Marion Pivonka Varga and Mrs. Agnes Zaicek Zabik for double-checking my Slovak and advising on Starenka's "olden days" stories. Na zdravie!

Dr. Ralph J. Yulo, professor emeritus, Eastern Connecticut State University, thank you for sharing your love of astronomy and ensuring the accuracy of the constellations visible in a Rhode Island sky in September.

Mrs. Kathryn Fitzgerald, sixth grade teacher extraordinaire, who continues to generously share her time, talent, and expertise on all things sixth grade and STEM (and Block Island too!), Thank you for reading an early draft of *Galaxy* to your students at Crystal Lake School in Ellington, Connecticut. I am forever grateful for the phenomenal advice I received from the most important critics of all!

Mr. Rob Gilpin, North Light commission

chair, New Shoreham, Rhode Island, thank you for exchanging numerous emails that helped me provide accurate details describing the beautiful and historic North Lighthouse.

Thank you to Ellington Middle School's technology education teacher, Mr. James Matroni, who reviewed last-minute details of the middle grade television studio to ensure its accuracy.

To my amazing galaxy of friends, who have shared their prayers, light, love, spirit, and many kindnesses throughout this journey, especially Sue Ferruolo, Deb Zulick, Sarah Zulick Sardo, Beverly McRory, Kim Covello DellaPorta, Jamie Covello, Maryann Covello Bastian, Roxanne Schirra, Margaret Morrison, Rachel Galligan, Lorie Williams, Michelle McClane, Kimi Moretti, Laurie Spruill, Kim Bocchino, Brandy Ambrosi, Anita Overgaard, Susan Wivell, Laura Shovan, Lynda Mullaly Hunt, Mary Pierce, Bette Anne Rieth, Kate Lynch, Pam Farley, Sam Gejdenson, Betsy Henley-Cohn, Andrea Adelman, Gail Bysiewicz, Maureen McGuire,

Peggy Strange, Liz Crutcher, Ann Morency, Crissy Goodin, and Kara Stanley.

I am so blessed to be part of an amazing family who makes my galaxy complete. Thank you, Barbara Yauch Zulick (aka Mom); Robert, Karen, Olivia, and John Zulick; Michelle and Isaac Trueblood; Deborah Zulick; Sarah Zulick Sardo; Avery and Hannah Sardo; John Ferruolo and Beverly McRory; Greg, Sue, Nick, and Mary Ferruolo; Kelly Owens; John and Jackie Ferruolo; Seth, Elizabeth, and Cru Coulter; and Thomas Ferruolo,

To my dear friends Hassan Salley and Yale Cantor. Thank you for inspiring characters who share your high values of empathy, generosity, and a sense of duty.

This book was written, revised, and edited while I received chemotherapy, radiation, and surgery to treat a rare but aggressive sarcoma. It is the true courage and compassion of the amazing doctors and nurses at Memorial Sloan Kettering Cancer Center that brought me through this journey, especially: Mary Louise Keohan, M.D.; Aimee Crago, M.D.; Annie Roth, R.N.; Kaled Alektiar, M.D.; and Jaspreet Sandhu, M.D. Every human should have access to the same incredible healthcare that I have been blessed to receive.

Most of all, thank you to my amazing children, Andrew and Sophia. You are the brightest stars in my galaxy. I didn't know how "impossibly big" love could be until I met you.

GOFISH

MEET THE WOMEN WHO SHAPED THE CHARACTER SITARA IN *A GALAXY OF SEA STARS*

While working on my first middle grade novel, *Ruby in the Sky*, I had the privilege of working with an amazing group of refugee youth through the organization IRIS—Integrated Refugee and Immigrant Services—in New Haven, Connecticut (irisct.org). These young men and women read an early version of *Ruby*, then met with me to offer their advice and suggestions for the character Ahmad Saleem, who was a refugee from Syria.

As the project wound down, members of the group asked me to recommend other books with refugee characters. It quickly became apparent that, although there are many wonderful books about refugees, there aren't nearly enough with refugee characters. From this realization, a new group formed, as five young women with roots in Afghanistan, Iraq, and Syria came together to help create such a book. The goal of this new project was to provide an opportunity for these ladies to reach out to the world to say: "This is what I want you to know about me, this is how it has been for us, and this is how we'd like it to be."

In the beginning, we met at IRIS, and I simply listened as they talked about their home countries as well as their wishes, dreams, and fears for their lives in the United

States. Their experiences spun together to shape the character Sitara Haidary. For more than a year, these young women read multiple versions of *A Galaxy of Sea Stars*, each time offering their critical insight and advice as the story developed.

From the moment I met these women, their bravery and courage inspired me, but I never fully expected how they would change my life. During this time, I faced a challenging cancer diagnosis, and our meetings were scheduled around surgeries, chemotherapy, and radiation. But for me, each time we reunited was like breathing new air, and I'd easily forget about everything else. The willingness of these ladies to invite me into their lives and homes and share their courageous optimism has inspired me in ways I can't describe. I can only say that each time I return to IRIS, it still feels something like coming home—an emotion that I think many people share.

I am so grateful for this opportunity for readers to get to know the inspiring young women who helped shape Sitara's story. Like me, I believe you will feel braver for knowing them.

1. Tell us a bit about yourself.
My name is **Hilla** and I am from Afghanistan. I came to the US when I was thirteen.

My name is **Deyana** and I am from Iraq, but I have also lived in Syria and Turkey. I came to the US when I was fifteen.

My name is **Nour** and I left Syria when I was eleven. I lived in Jordan as a refugee and then came to the US when I was fifteen.

My name is **Maria** and I am from Afghanistan. I came to the US when I was twenty.

My name is **Safia** and I am from Afghanistan. I came to the US when I was eighteen.

My name is **Asma** and my family is from Afghanistan. I was the first child in my family born in the United States.

2. If it weren't for each one of you, *A Galaxy of Sea Stars* would never have become a book! How did you feel about working on this project?
Deyana: This was my first time experiencing a story about a refugee. Working on this project gave me comfort because it was an opportunity to describe many feelings I experienced as a refugee coming to a new country.

Asma: I enjoyed being part of this project because it made me think of myself when I was Izzy's and Sitara's ages. Whenever our middle school cafeteria felt too loud, I escaped into books and reimagined myself as those heroines with simple, easy-to-pronounce names, who possessed the kind of courage I wanted for myself. But the girls in those books were not like me. Each night, I'd wonder whether those characters ever knew what it was like to occupy the lonely space between two worlds, as I did. If twelve-year-old Asma had brought *A Galaxy of Sea Stars* to the cafeteria with her, I think she would have seen parts of herself in both Sitara and Izzy. I also think she would have been inspired to put the book down and talk to other kids, because then she would have recognized the power of girls like her.

Hilla: Sometimes in school when I talked about Afghanistan, my classmates didn't believe me. They had this wrong idea of what they *thought* Afghanistan was like so stuck in their heads from what they'd seen on TV or in the movies that they wouldn't listen to someone who'd actually lived there. Working on this project, I shared many facts about my country and my culture with people interested in really learning about Afghanistan. For example, in the melmastiyâ scene, readers can see how important family is to Afghans and how generosity is a big part of Afghan culture.

Nour: It was important for me to work on this project and share parts of my own story so that *A Galaxy of Sea Stars* would accurately represent one of the many hidden stories that need to be told about immigrant and refugee struggles.

3. What is something that you want readers to know about your home country?

Deyana: In the US, people are always telling me that my country, Iraq, is destroyed and that we don't have things such as restaurants, movie theaters, parks, and museums. I want people to know that Iraq is a beautiful country with a rich culture and history. Iraq is the birthplace to some of the world's earliest known civilizations. There are many historical places to visit like Sami Abdulrahman Park, the Kurdish Textile Museum, Lalish, and Shanadar Park. Iraq is known for many famous poets, painters, and sculptors.

Asma: Although there have been many years of war in Afghanistan, we are far from a broken people. Afghans are astronomers, poets, scientists, scholars, storytellers, and individuals. My ancestor Ahmad Shah Durrānī was as much a poet as he was a king. I grew up on stories of

Kabul's bustling streets, the emerald pastures of Logar, and summer nights spent naming constellations. Together, these stories convey the image of a country that is simultaneously ordinary and extraordinary, as well as unabashedly alive. Despite all they may be going through, an Afghan will not let you leave their home with an empty stomach; after making you eat as much as you possibly can, they will also ensure you have more than enough to take home. I know no better indication of a beautiful life than that.

Nour: Syria, also known as the "Country of Jasmine," has the friendliest and most hospitable people. In Syria you will find a mosque next to a church next to a synagogue. Our neighbors were of all faiths, but Syrian people don't care about what religion you are as much as who you are inside. In Syria, being friendly and kind to each other is more important than anything.

4. What was the hardest part about leaving your home and coming to the United States?

Deyana: When I was six, my family moved to Syria. Even though Arabic is spoken there, it was very different than the dialect I'd grown up with in Iraq. Then we moved to Turkey and I had to learn Turkish. When we came to the US, I then had to learn a third language—English. I came in the ninth grade, and there were so many students in my high school—it was like a sea of faces to me. Everyone was a stranger; the hallways were completely foreign. Even though I already knew two languages, English was so hard because it is read the opposite of Arabic (which is read right to left) and has completely different characters for its alphabet and numbers. For the first six months, I didn't understand anything my teachers were saying. I couldn't read road signs or understand my classmates. I was afraid to speak because even one letter in one word can change the entire meaning of what you are trying to say. If I said something wrong, sometimes people laughed at me, so I was afraid to speak. I felt like I couldn't learn. Inside me I felt very lost and alone.

Hilla: When I was leaving Afghanistan, I didn't really understand everything that meant. But when I got to the United States, my aunt immediately came to my mind. Right then, I realized how much I would miss her and how I may never see her in person again. That is when everything became more real to me. It was very hard.

Nour: We had to leave many family members behind. It was especially hard to leave my uncle and his family because he was so much like a father to me—I even called him Baba (Dad).

5. In *A Galaxy of Sea Stars*, some kids are unkind to Sitara because she wears hijab. Have you ever been treated differently because you wear hijab? How did that make you feel?

Deyana: During Ramadan, I came to school wearing hijab, and a classmate told me I should take it off because I look "more beautiful" without it. This upset me because my friend was not understanding that hijab is not just a piece of cloth to me—it is my faith. It is who I am. This person thought they were giving me a compliment, but their words hurt me.

Nour: On more than one occasion, I have been harassed for wearing hijab. Statistics show that women are more often a target because of hijab. I have been yelled at many times and told to go back to my country. This has happened more than once in train stations as I've traveled to and from college, where I major in physiology and neurobiology and am on the premed track. I'm not sure what right anyone has to tell anyone else where they should go.

Hilla: One time a classmate asked me about hijab, but she asked it in a really nice and respectful way. She wanted to learn more about why I wore hijab. I loved the way she asked, and I was happy to answer her questions.

6. Are there other ways you have been treated differently? What advice can you offer other kids who might be feeling the same way?

Deyana: One time an adviser kept pushing me to go to a certain school because she said that it was better for students like me, who had learned English as a second language. But I didn't want to go to that school. My English was strong, and I was interested in other schools. But it didn't matter to her. She would only listen to what she thought was best for me, not what I knew was best for me. Being kind requires that we not only listen to each other, but really hear each other, understand new perspectives, and show respect for them.

Asma: I will never know what it is to be a refugee, but I do know what it is like to be treated differently. I know that the distinct pain of being told to "go back home" never dulls, no matter how much time has passed since you first had to redefine what home means. I also know that kindred spirits exist the world over. It is okay to share your story with those who want to understand, and it is okay—always—to correct mispronunciations of your name, even if it takes several tries.

7. At the end of the story, Izzy and Sitara go on the school news to talk about their fathers' experiences working with the United States in Afghanistan. Why was this scene important to you and why do you think it was important for the story?

Hilla: Many Afghans have come to the United States through the Special Immigrant Visa (SIV) Program, which Sitara talks about in this scene. I think many Americans don't know that people who come through SIV have worked to help the United States in their countries, or that their families were in serious danger because of that work. This is the reality for many Afghans, so to not mention it would be like hiding the truth. I liked how Izzy and Sitara shared this with their school because it is also a part of my history and something I am proud of.

Asma: By sharing their experiences, Izzy and Sitara taught their classmates about something they knew nothing about. But mostly, this scene matters to me because it provided both girls an opportunity to claim how *they* were impacted by what their fathers had endured. Owning these truths in front of the entire school showed how brave they truly were. And from their courage sprung another truth: Although we feel more comfortable when we understand one another, our ability to be kind does not depend on this. Our choice to be kind shouldn't either.

Nour: I loved how Sitara inspires Izzy to speak up and do the news. This scene also shows the friendship that they built and how they became stronger together. Each one of us is unique in some way—we don't all look the same or do the same things. Our world has many scars and we need people like Sitara and Izzy to speak up so they can be healed.

Maria & Safia: In our country we have seen war. The things American kids have seen in movies, we have seen with our own eyes. It is horrible. We came to the United States with many wishes for a better life. But when we first came it seemed as if many of these wishes would never come true. It was so hard to not understand the language and we were very lonely. When Sitara tells her story, she is also telling our story so that hopefully readers will understand more about us and our lives.

8. Why do you think American-born kids should read this story, and what can they learn from it?

Nour: I hope readers will understand what it is like to be a refugee. For refugees, the first week you are in the United States is one of the hardest times you will face. Imagine that you are seven years old and you are walking with your mom in a busy place, like Times Square in New York City, and all of a sudden you have lost your mom's hand. You are looking around, and people are racing by, and no one is looking down to see you there or notice that you are crying and need help. That feeling represents what it is like when you first come to the United States as a refugee. You will not always find people who understand you and where you have come from. Sometimes the wrong person will get in your face and make fun of you because you don't speak English. For many refugees, it can make them feel discouraged and make them think that they should give up and go back to the wars and struggles they've just escaped.

Hilla: A lot of people think that girls who wear hijab are being forced to or that their parents are making them wear it. I want to wear hijab because of my faith. It is important for people to understand that it is our personal choice to wear hijab.

Asma: I think readers can learn from this book that creating a space for others to speak can be as powerful as using your own voice. This might mean asking someone about the book they've brought with them to the cafeteria, especially if they are sitting alone. It also means knowing that a person may not want to answer your question. We all make mistakes, but that is not an excuse to not try to understand each other and how we are all different. Anything worth doing, believing in, and fighting for is always going to be scary because it needs to be. I have followed this truth to the front of classrooms, to the center of difficult conversations, and eventually to podiums. It is because of this that I raise my hand as high as I can to answer questions about myself and Afghanistan—especially when my hand is bright red with henna!

9. Is there something refugee kids can learn from Izzy and Sitara's story? What do you think that is and why?

Safia: When I first came to this country, I didn't know English and couldn't defend myself with words—so when I didn't understand something, I would apologize to people even though I hadn't done anything wrong. I liked the way Sitara never apologized. She also was brave in making new friends, which is a very hard thing to do when English isn't your first language.

Hilla: I think that many refugee kids go through similar things that Sitara experienced, because of the way they dress or speak differently. Reading about how Sitara dealt with these challenges could be like a guide, where kids could see how she faced the same situations with pride. Also, when you see someone else going through something you have had to face, it can make you feel less alone.

Asma: I think that all kinds of kids can learn about what it means to find "home" from Izzy and Sitara's story. My best friend Sophie's family immigrated to the US from France and Poland. When her family visited mine for tea, my mom woke up early to prepare as extensively as she knew how. Sophie's grandmother complimented the *halwa* in French, my mom responded in Dari, and in the midst of our shared translation I realized that maybe home isn't actually a place. Maybe home is being with those who try their best to understand you, and who love you for all of who you are.

10. The experiences and advice each of you shared on this project shaped the character Sitara—but still, she is her own person. Is there anything about Sitara that inspired you or that you admire?

Safia: Sometimes at my work I meet police officers, and from them I realized that I want to be a police officer, too, someday. But I thought that I couldn't do that job because I wear hijab. In the story, Sitara was very proud to wear hijab, and so am I. From working on and talking about the book, I realized that I can wear hijab everywhere, especially as a police officer.

Asma: Sitara skips across rooftops, ventures into the sea, raises her hand in class, shares her story with the entire school, and feels angry, alone, and afraid. Sitara is Sitara, and that is what I admire most about her. And when Izzy doesn't initially understand her, Sitara doesn't change so that she can. Instead she inspires Izzy to want to be more like her—brave and strong.

Hilla: I liked how Sitara always spoke up for herself. When I was new to my school and someone would say something offensive, I would do my best to ignore it. But Sitara reminded me to be more willing to speak up. She made me realize that you don't have to get into an argument or go down to their level when you respond—just stay positive.

Nour: I like how brave Sitara is in the story, and I think that most kids who come to a new country have to find this kind of courage. One of the bravest things I ever had to do was to say "stop" to a student who was making fun of a kid who had been in the US for less than a week. It was hard to see the same thing happening again and again, and nobody doing anything about it. Saying "stop" may seem like a very simple or easy thing to do for many people, but it is not. It actually takes a lot of courage. I believe that lots of kids, coming from many different experiences, who read *A Galaxy of Sea Stars* will gain courage to speak up and tell their stories and stop accepting unkind and offensive treatment because of the way they look or where they are from.

11. What was your favorite scene in *A Galaxy of Sea Stars* and why?
Hilla: My favorite scene was when Izzy and Sitara did the news together at the end of the story. A lot of the kids had made assumptions about Sitara, and I liked how she spoke up for herself and said who she really was.

Deyana: My favorite scene was when Sitara spoke for the first time on the school news about wearing hijab, because it was an essential part of making her classmates understand why and how important it is to her. This was a very courageous thing to do.

Asma: Because I, too, dream of becoming a lawyer-astronomer (I'm working on the lawyer part right now, but I'll get to the rest!), my favorite scene in the story is when Izzy and Sitara "journey to Narnia." Growing up, my answer to the question of what I wanted to become ranged from pediatrician, teacher, journalist, and wildlife photographer to engineer, novelist, lawyer, and world-shaker (whose job it would be to stand behind podiums and rouse audiences to action!). Like Izzy and Sitara, I feel large when I consider all that I can be, but also small when I look into the night sky. Like Izzy and Sitara, I see the connection between our individual stories, aspirations, and identities and how— like the constellations they gaze at from their rooftop—this understanding can illuminate our way forward.

Nour: My favorite scene is when Izzy and Sitara do the news together, because it shows how when one person has the courage to speak up, it will inspire others to speak up, too—and that together these voices can change minds and make a positive impact.

12. Are there any last thoughts, ideas, or advice you would like to leave with readers?

Deyana: I want to say that there should be more books with refugee characters. These types of stories can create a significant and positive opportunity to understand the experiences of many refugees.

Asma: The first time I gave a speech in front of my class-mates, I remember praying that no one would notice my hands trembling behind the podium. I'd written about why we must know the shared history of our world, and I began my speech as I begin every important task. First I said, "Bismillah"—in the name of God. Then, with the same breath, I said, "let your courage be bigger than your fear." The shaking didn't stop, but my voice began. I am grateful I could contribute to a story that represents this reality. If I could tell twelve-year-old me that a character would one day come to embody some of what she was, I know she would hold her head higher. Twenty-year-old me certainly does.

Nour: I never imagined I would have the opportunity of be-ing a consultant on a project like this. I have been inspired by every part of the process, starting from day one to the day I saw the result. And by the result, I do not mean the day the book was published—but the day people have read this book and had the chance to understand more about what it means to be a refugee.

Safia: My advice to readers would be to go out of your way to be friends and be kind to new kids. Make them not feel like a stranger. Kindness belongs to everyone.

Maria: I would like to say that it is important to always be kind to each other, because you don't know what other people have gone through.